ALI AND
RAMAZAN

Also by Perihan Magden:

Escape (forthcoming)
Two Girls
The Messenger Boy Murders

ALI AND RAMAZAN

PERIHAN MAGDEN
TRANSLATED BY RUTH WHITEHOUSE

amazon crossing

Text copyright © 2009 by Perihan Magden
English translation copyright © 2012 by Ruth Whitehouse

Ali and Ramazan by Perihan Magden was first published in 2009 by Doğan Kin, in Istanbul, as *Ali ile Ramazan*.

Translated from the Turkish by Ruth Whitehouse.
First published in English in 2012 by AmazonCrossing.

Published by AmazonCrossing
P.O. Box 400818
Las Vegas, NV 89140

ISBN-13: 9781611091410
ISBN-10: 1611091411
Library of Congress Control Number: 2011917262

There was nobody to care for those two
children: Ali and Ramazan.

To my dear friend, Barbaros Altuğ, who insisted
that I continued to care about those children
who were constantly on my mind.

Based on a true story

THE COURTYARD

Ali appeared at the orphanage one day. In the stone courtyard. But the children called it a garden. They always referred to the stone courtyard as the garden. The mosque courtyard was large, but the orphanage only had a crooked little piece of a madrasa courtyard behind a mosque. Most of the madrasa courtyard was incorporated into the mosque courtyard, but right at the back, beyond the triangle in the far corner, there was a sort of arrow-shaped area that had been set aside for the orphanage. It was a place for the children to play outside and do what they wanted.

The orphanage had been converted from the old madrasa, and Ramazan had been there for years. For years, he had been saying to his friends, "Let's play marbles in the garden." Ramazan was crazy about marbles. He played really well; there was nothing mediocre about the way he played. Not a kid at the orphanage could beat him. The same went for outside. No one had ever managed to beat Ramazan at marbles. At the far end of the stone courtyard was a stretch of earth the length of the wall. It was a thin strip of soil that had been left untouched on account of

1

a few old trees. That was the real garden. Maybe it was because of Ramazan and his passion for that ribbon of earth that the children always referred to the courtyard as the garden. Ramazan's soul burrowed along that ribbon of earth like a mole. With his hands, he made hollows big enough to punch a fist into. These hollows were for games of marbles. Ramazan liked playing *kuyu* and *çukur* best. They were the most difficult games. Ramazan loved to show off his skill. And winning—he loved the feeling of euphoria it gave him. "I beat all of you! You can't beat me at marbles, you idiots!" It was his only success in life, and he could not get enough of it. Even if he could not play marbles when at school, out and about, or asleep, his hands would be making the motions, his fingers constantly moving as if playing marbles. He could not help it. A few times a week, he would hand out marbles to the better players at the orphanage, safe in the knowledge that he was bound to win them all back anyway. He also handed out the ones he won from kids outside the orphanage, making sure to give away his favorites, the rarest and most perfect marbles, just to taste the pleasure of winning them back again. Ramazan wanted to spend his life winning and enjoying the pleasure of winning. But that was only possible when playing marbles.

It was cold that day. The children pestered him to go and play *üçgen*, a game he found boring. "That's kids' stuff! Stop bothering me." Then he smiled, showing his lovely teeth. "Come on then, have a go. I'll beat you all at *üçgen* as well!" The moment they started playing, he was in the lead. He ended up beating them all. "So much for *üçgen*!" he said, bending down to gather up his winnings. What a great feeling, and he had not even been trying. He rolled the marble he had given to Recep two days before, following it with his eyes and gazing at the beautiful blues whirling around inside it. The marble stopped under a foot covered with rubber. A huge foot. It was not wearing a shoe or a boot, but two pieces of rubber from a truck tire tied up with string.

"Shit!" Ramazan said between his teeth. "Who the hell are you? Gimme that marble!" A child he had never seen before bent down and took the marble from under his foot. He put it in the palms of his hands and held out his enormous arms to Ramazan.

"Hey, who are you? How did you get here at this time of night?"

"I'm Ali," said the boy with the long arms and huge hands. He was at least two heads taller than Ramazan. "The police just brought me here." He was swallowing hard to fight back tears. He looked upward, his eyes fixed on the darkness of the courtyard.

"Well, they call me Boss around here. We'll call you Caoutchouc. What are those on your feet? Have you come down from the mountains, Cave-boy?"

The children in the garden all laughed, partly to please Ramazan and partly because of their unease about the hugeness of this new boy. Ali put his head to one side. "OK, Boss." He was still swallowing hard, and the tremble in his voice was only partly due to the cold.

"Good on you, man!" said Ramazan, giving Ali a slap on the back of his head. Ali had to be kept in place after all. He suddenly felt cheered by the possibility that Old Rubber Shoes might provide him with a new challenge at marbles. "Hey, Caoutchouc, you any good at marbles?"

"What, Boss?"

"I'm talking about these." Ramazan took some marbles out of his pocket and showed them to Ali.

"We don't have any of those where I live. We play with fruit stones." This giant of a child had a strange way of talking. He

3

produced sounds from deep in his throat, hoarse and guttural; he spoke as if talking in another language, not Turkish. "Let me have this one and I'll play." Ali was looking in amazement at the marble in his hand.

"You're all right, Ali man; take it, the marble's yours! But if you can't play right, I'll punch you in the head." The moment Ramazan uttered those words, he wondered if he had gone too far with this giant kid, because the mountain monster could have him on the ground in no time if he chose to.

"Thanks, Boss," said the giant kid. His eyes were still darting about, looking this way and that. Ramazan was bewildered to see that Ali seemed to have tears in his eyes. If this mountain monster ever insisted on being called boss, it would be very embarrassing. The other kids would never listen to him again. "He's as big a bear. He must have come down from the mountain forests with those rubber feet. I'll have that jerk in the palm of my hand, and I'll make sure I keep him there," thought Ramazan to himself as he darted into the orphanage. How long would he keep Ali in the palm of his hand? How tightly would he hold him there? He did not yet know. Ramazan knew nothing yet. Nothing at all.

ALI 2

Ali arrived at the orphanage when the cold was first starting to bite. Yes, it was cold, but not that cold yet. When you thought of the orphanage, you immediately thought of cold, the coldness of stone. It was a vast place with no furniture or carpets, a place that made you shiver inside from top to toe. It made you shrink, cower, and withdraw into yourself.

Ramazan knew for a fact that an orphanage meant coldness. Being an orphan meant being cold. You were always cold, so there was no point shivering. "Shivering doesn't stop you feeling cold," he kept saying to Ali. The mountain monster shivered all day, for weeks, for months. His teeth chattered. The noise of his teeth rattling really got on Ramazan's nerves. When scolded about it, Ali would say in a tearful voice, "OK, Boss. I promise I'll stop shivering. It's not really so cold today, is it?"

Ali had close-shaven curly hair. His hair was so thick and strong that it did not appear curly unless you looked very closely. Ramazan would go and stand right under Ali's nose and look at him long and hard. He made no secret of it; he just stood there and stared. Ali had a beautiful, broad nose. It was a small nose that came straight down and flared at the nostrils. It was not like any nose he had seen before. "Hey, Caoutchouc!" said Ramazan. "Jungle-boy, what kind of nose is that? There aren't any like that around here."

Ali had large, pitch-black eyes that slanted slightly. They were the darkest eyes Ramazan had ever seen, the color of night, coal, or dark olives. Ali was a chubby-cheeked child, with full lips. The way his large lower lip drooped made him look sad, absentminded, as if in a trance. His eyes kept welling up. For the first days, first months, first years, his eyes were always welling up.

And he shivered. Ali shivered for years. The shivering did not stop until he started taking solvents.

Ali's skin was dark and smooth, a flawless deep brown. Ramazan put his hand next to Ali's, and Ali recoiled. Fearfully, he snatched his hand away and hid it in the pocket of his outgrown navy-blue trousers. "Are you an Arab, or what? Look at that dark color. Your nose and everything about you is weird, man."

"I'm an Arab, Boss. We're Nusayris: Arab Alevis."

"Hey, Fellah! We needed a fellah, we're complete now you're here." Ramazan started laughing. Actually, he was laughing at himself because he was completely smitten by Ali. He could not stop himself from running up to him all the time. One day he would say Fellah, then Caoutchouc, Mountain-monster, Caveboy, or Jungle-boy. He kept giving him names, anything he could think of. Ali enjoyed being given names by this boss who was only a year older than himself; he enjoyed being teased like a beetle under a magnifying glass. But Ali was not cowed by anything that irritating, brazen kid did; he even felt a strange, inexplicable sense of gratitude for the interest taken in him. Ramazan would always fix on new boys. He worked on them, chewed them up, and tore them to pieces, but only for a couple of weeks, maybe three or four. Then, he would get bored and spit them out like tobacco that has lost its taste. But everything about this dark giant of a boy fascinated him.

The other boys looked on in amazement. They understood straightaway, with wordless recognition, that Ali and Ramazan complemented each other perfectly. They did not need to talk; they just felt each other's mood. But that was only the start. Ali and Ramazan were only just starting. Ramazan taught Ali how to play marbles. Ali understood the numbering of the glass balls immediately, and he grasped the games quickly. His body somehow did everything with a rare grace, making it look easy. Ali spoke faster than anyone else. He climbed trees skillfully. He could lift the heaviest loads, carrying them as if they weighed nothing at all. And he started to play marbles very well. When he wanted to, he played better than Ramazan, but only if he wanted to because he did not care about winning. Ali did not care about that; he had no appetite for it, no desire. He would clamber like a cat to the top of a tree, and then sit motionless. His lower lip would droop, and he would look sad, as if to say "What am I looking for? What am I doing here? Who am I?" At moments like that, Ramazan had to remind Ali where he was and what he was supposed to be doing: "Hey, come down! Are you going to spend all year up there, Jungle-bear?"

Ali came from a village near Samandağ in Hatay province. He never said what the name of the village was. He said his father was a fisherman who drank a lot. He drank and drank, and was always beating Ali and his mother. He would beat anyone he could lay his hands on. For those dreadful beatings, he used terrible things. He would use unimaginable things to hit the poor wretches, without any sign of remorse. Ali was injured, his mother left disabled. One day, his mother struck his father on the head with a pickaxe that she had hidden away. She split his father's head in two in front of Ali. Right there on the floor where the meal was laid out. Then, she swallowed some agricultural chemical and locked herself in the next room. She suffered a long and painful death, convulsing for hours with foam oozing from her nose and mouth. Ali had remained sitting on the floor in front of the food. In the center of the tablecloth, right next to the cold, semi-congealed soup, was his father's split head with the pickaxe still in the middle of it. From the next room his mother could be heard moaning as she writhed about. Ali had done nothing; he had remained motionless. Because he knew that neither his mother's nor his father's family wanted him.

But Ali did not explain all that. Ramazan found answers to his questions by making Master read out Ali's file to him. Ramazan was not sure if Ali remembered all these things. He seemed to have cauterized his soul to stop the pain. That was why, when asked a question, he did not answer but just looked this way and that. Ramazan was surprised that, out of so many boys with awful stories to tell, Ali was so affected by what had happened to him. Ramazan was surprised that, instead of losing interest as he usually did, he continued to put up with Ali. He kept resorting to teasing mode. "Our Fellah is a sensitive fellah," he would say, making as if to give Ali a slap. "Did they put a sparrow or something inside that huge body of yours? What did they do to you, man? Our Caoutchouc never stops shivering!" Ali would respond to Ramazan's nonsensical provocations by smiling and revealing pearly-white teeth that contrasted with his dark skin.

Something about Ramazan's interest was good for Ali. He felt as if a cauldron of cold water had been poured over the burning sensation inside him, as if a quilt of down had been spread over his shivering body. Ramazan was good for Ali.

He did not know the words for what was happening to him, but he was falling in love. Ali was falling head-over-heels in love. As far as it was possible to fall.

RAMAZAN 3

Ramazan was like a child in a Turkish film. That was what he kept telling himself. "You wouldn't believe it if I told you my story, Caoutchouc! You'd say it could be the story of a kid in a Turkish movie. An imam found me in the courtyard of a mosque when he went to make the morning call to prayer. What about that, eh?" said Ramazan, chuckling like a cat, as though he had just given a very amusing self-introduction. Ramazan had a genuine laugh, which started from his stomach and enveloped his whole being. He also had a variety of artificial grins. Ali learned to recognize the smiling face Ramazan adopted when he wanted something, or when he wanted to persuade somebody to do something for him that was impossible. He also learned to recognize Ramazan's catlike grin and all the other artificial smiles. He memorized them all and fixed them firmly in his mind.

Ramazan knew he was beautiful and bright; he had been since infancy. And he knew how much it suited him to smile. He even knew the magic of turning slightly to the right to show off his best and most handsome side. People would give him whatever he asked for. They could not resist him; he knew that. Ramazan had been found as an infant in swaddling clothes in a mosque courtyard and taken to the local police station; ever since then, he had relied on his beauty and sparkle to satisfy his needs. When the imam had finished his call to prayer, he and his wife took the swaddled infant to the police station. The imam was terrified his wife would say, "Let's keep this baby," because they had no children of their own. At the police station, the men were delighted with the smiling pink-and-white infant in his pure white swaddling clothes. Like an adorable baby poster! The imam's fears were not unfounded: his wife sobbed uncontrollably as they handed him over. The imam's wife insisted on the police naming him Ramazan, because it was just two days before the start of the holy month of Ramazan. "So you see, if I'd been found on Victory Day, I'd have been called Zafer," said Ramazan with his catlike chuckle. Ramazan tried to joke about how he was named, yet he was a true orphan. Where he came from was totally unknown; whose child he was would never be known. Ramazan lived with the stigma of belonging to no one. The police took him to the nearby Darülaceze Poorhouse Nursery so that they could visit him occasionally; they named the lovely baby as the imam's wife had requested. Most of the babies cared for at the Darülaceze were very handicapped with no chance of being adopted; any prospective parents would rather die than take home a crippled child. For Ramazan, his innate beauty and sparkle were both his fortune and his damnation.

Then Master arrived on the scene. Of course, he was not a principal at that stage, merely a member of the staff. Ramazan could not stay at the Darülaceze nursery beyond the age of five, so he was sent to Maltepe Children's Home, where Master was the deputy principal. From then on, wherever Master went,

Ramazan went, too. The moment Master was appointed to a new orphanage, he ensured Ramazan was transferred there with him before even finding a place to live or a school for his daughters. Master adored Ramazan as if he were his own flesh and blood. He would not even entertain the idea of going to a different orphanage if Ramazan was not there. That was why he insisted on staying where he was, refusing to be sent out to Anatolia during the years when his charismatic, successful peers were moving up the professional ladder. At least, that's what he told his drinking pals. Yes, he could have been promoted to more important posts in Ankara. However, for Master, it was much more important, crucial even, that he did not leave Istanbul, or Ramazan. Ramazan used to imagine that he was the son of a rich woman because, as Master had repeatedly told him with tears in his eyes, he was found in the courtyard of a mosque in a good area. He was a healthy, smiling baby dressed in pure white swaddling clothes. Ramazan used to imagine that his mother had abandoned him because of her family, and that one day she would arrive at the orphanage door in a large luxury car. It would be like a Turkish film, and she would be played by Türkan Şoray. A chauffeur would open the car door; she would get out and run to embrace him, crying, "Orçun, my darling!" (or some other name used for rich kids in Turkish films). Then, finally, she would rescue him from the orphanage, the destitution, the cold, the deprivation, and from Master.

Actually, Ramazan liked the idea of being a child in a Turkish film. It made him feel proud. His story had no certainties like that of Ali, who knew where he came from and who his family was. He had not been thrown out like a piece of garbage. Ali's mother died in agony, and his father was split in two. His mother's family did not want him because he had not saved his mother, and his father's family did not want him because he had not saved his father. Ali was a pathetic peasant kid from an impoverished village. What could his story lead to? Could it save him from the dead end of orphanage life? Could Ali have any sort of happy ending? For Ramazan, however, it was possible that his father was a very rich man and his mother had been too proud to tell him about Ramazan. One day, she would be unable to bear it any longer. "Orçun, I have something to tell you," she would feel compelled to say. "We have a son I've kept secret from you all this time." His father (yes, his name was also Orçun) would hit his mother. He would be furious and unable to control his anger; he would grab her by the hair and send her sprawling to the floor. He would lash out at her because she had abandoned their baby and kick her in the face because she did not tell him about their son for so long. Blood would run from his mother's mouth and nose, and her broken teeth would be scattered across the floor.

Serves her right! She left her baby in a mosque courtyard without even telling his father. She turned Ramazan into an orphanage kid. Serves her right! Then his father would race to the orphanage in his Mercedes. He would leave it in the middle of the street, run inside, and go straight to Master's room. Oh yes, that's where he would head for.

He would give Master one on the chin. Then another one, and another. He would get hold of Master's head and shove it through the windowpane. Pieces of glass would rip Master's face to shreds, and a shard would press against his throat like a knife. As soon as he had finished with Master, he would run out into the garden and, the moment he saw Ramazan, would cry out, "My son!" He would recognize his son Orçun instantly because father and son would look so alike.

"My son! Orçun! I swear, I had no idea of your existence. That mother of yours told me nothing! But now I realize I've been waiting for this moment all my life. All my life, my dear son, for you!"

"Me too, Father," Ramazan, or rather Orçun, would say. "Me too, Father. Me too, Father. Me too. Waiting for you has kept me going. I never gave up. I always kept going. Always, Father. Oh my dear Father!"

"Boss, are you all right? Are you sleepy? You weren't in your bed last night." They were supposed to be doing their homework in the study. Ali was prodding Ramazan gently. He was worried because he had never seen Ramazan like this.

"I'm fine, couldn't be better. I'm on top of the world." Ramazan started to laugh heartily. He was going to get out of there. His days there were numbered. Ali laughed with him. Whenever Ramazan cheered up, it made Ali feel happy. Ramazan's feelings would have an immediate effect on Ali, as if they were twins. But not the other way around. Ali adopted whatever mood Ramazan was in. All his feelings changed according to Ramazan. Whichever way the wind blew for Ramazan, Ali was blown in the same direction.

THE ORPHANAGE

The orphanage brought to mind stone and cold, the coldness of stone, stone coldness. And filth. Unbelievable filth. Layer upon layer of dreadful filth. It was dirt that was permanent and constant, that did not go away and never would. The fat old woman who cooked the meals and was responsible for cleaning the kitchen had grown fat from being idle and useless. Some of the children actually called her Mother or Granny. No way! Ramazan would never say Mother or Granny to that filthy old woman. He called her Aunt Nezahat, but only if he had to, and it always stuck in his throat. He hated Aunt Nezahat because she made disgusting meals and was filthy. He hated her for her dirtiness and indolence. Aunt Nezahat refused to retire and disappear. If only she would go, she might be replaced by someone young and clean; perhaps then they would not have to live in such a shithole.

In Ramazan's eyes, Aunt Nezahat represented the state of the orphanage. Because of her indolence and dirty habits and because of the revolting gruel of flour and water she dished up three times a day, the two cleaners at the orphanage made no effort either. The toilets brought sewage into the area where the children poured water over themselves, which was the nearest they ever got to taking a bath. Actual sewage.

Two young men took it in turns to come and help the children with their studies; they were both bone idle, too. Then there was Şener, Master's assistant. Phantom Şener. There was nothing to say about him. The only thing he ever said was, "Yes, Master. As you say, Master."

Şener would look into Master's eyes, and his mood would change according to that of Master. Whenever Master was in the mood for singing and dancing, Şener would warble away idiotically. Whenever Master went off on a trip of self-pity, Phantom Şener would disappear and sit quietly in his room, where he would try to become invisible by blending into the walls and furniture.

There were two other members of staff, but no one knew what they were supposed to do. They did not know themselves. Fine, so there was nobody at the orphanage who actually did anything right. The moment the boys reached eighteen, the State turned them out onto the street, yet members of the orphanage staff were allowed to remain. They stayed at the orphanage doing sweet nothing except for marking the days, just waiting for the day they qualified for their pension. Tucking lank strands of hair into her dark green headscarf, Aunt Nezahat coughed, sneezed, and scratched as she dished out the disgusting broth, which they had to eat to avoid dying of starvation. She was finished and on her way home by half-past three, four o'clock at the latest. She left without clearing up that hellhole of a kitchen. She would go home early feeling exhausted, dragging her feet with fatigue. The next day, she would add yet another layer of filth to the festering, congealed layers of grease, scraps, and leftovers.

The filth in the kitchen was indescribable. It seemed to permeate the whole orphanage, along with the cockroaches and rats. The dormitories were filthy, as were the study rooms and the common room where they watched television. For some reason, Master called it the "lounge." The term "study room" was also his invention. When all the plates and cutlery were cleared away, the place where they ate became the study room. Just as it was far too grand to call the place where they ate the dining room, it irked Ramazan that the dump they lived in was called the orphanage.

As far as Ramazan was concerned, the place was no more than a children's jail or children's poorhouse that had been converted out of an old madrasa in the corner of a mosque courtyard, where seventy to eighty boys were just about kept alive. It was all Master's fault! Ramazan, unable to cope with his anger, blamed Master for all the decay and neglect at the orphanage.

Master never rebuked Aunt Nezahat or the two cleaners, who were so lazy they seemed barely able to walk. He never chided the tutors or the pointless Phantom Şener. Master just wanted to be left alone, without anyone bothering him. Thus, Master ensured he kept his seventy or eighty boys in that frightful limbo of a place until they were eighteen, without lifting a finger to do anything. He lived in his own miserable world, crying over regrets and personal crises.

The only thing that concerned him was where did it all go wrong? Maltepe Children's Home had not been like this. It had been fairly clean, with real meals and real beds. The tutors used to help the children finish their homework and were always ready to answer questions. The children washed once a week without fail; their clothes were laundered regularly, and outgrown clothes were replaced. In those days, Master was not quite so deranged, but his breath already smelled of drink. He used to try to cover it up with cloves, parsley, or cologne.

Because he was working under the eagle eye of a principal who saw everything, he kept his drinking habits and debauchery under control. Then, when Ramazan was nine years old, Master was promoted to the rank of principal and sent to this makeshift place converted from a ruined madrasa hidden at the back of a mosque courtyard.

Ramazan had been in this filthy place for four years because of Master. Who knew what might have happened if Master had not brought him here. Maybe he would have been a real primary school student in Maltepe. He would not have had so much hate for school and the world. He would not have been going out of his mind with loneliness. Ramazan always remembered Maltepe as a paradise from which he had been driven out. He cursed Master's obsession with him; yet, as he was only too conscious, he had played a considerable part in Master's excesses.

"Ramazan!" he would scold himself. "You sold yourself for pickings from Master's dinner table." Or maybe it was for a jacket or a pair of shoes. "You're the real reason why this man has stooped so low! You're to blame, not the bloody orphanage." When he reproached himself like that, his mind would suddenly turn to marbles. He would think of strikes he had made in his last game, about the kids he had beaten, his winnings, the bargains he had made, or his American trophies.

Then he would hurl himself out into the street and play marbles for hours. When the other children returned to their respective homes, he would rush back to the orphanage yard and, in an attempt to forget Master, his own failings, the filth of the orphanage, and the revolting meals, plead with the other boys, crying, "One more game, please, just one more." Ramazan wanted to forget he was an orphanage kid and be happy all the time. "Happy days pass quickly," he used to say. But the place was a prison, a jailhouse for orphans. He had turned thirteen, and he knew he was going from bad to worse. He had been buried in this hole of an orphanage with Master for thirteen times three hundred and sixty-five days! Was that mother of his ever going to come and rescue him? Was his rich bastard of a father ever going to come and take him away from this place? How much longer would they pretend Ramazan did not exist? After all, was he not Orçun? Their one and only son? But Orçun was fading, he was about to disappear. He was now thirteen. In the end, only Ramazan would remain. And then there was only Ramazan. Ramazan, the pathetic little orphan! A pitiful bit of filth who sold himself! Ramazan was as bad as the filthy, disgusting orphanage. That is the way it was. It was not that Ramazan did not know. He knew very well what had happened to him. That was why he needed Ali. He needed someone to make him feel clean, to cleanse his soul with love.

GHOUL 5

Master began to sense that something was going on. But he realized this later than the orphanage boys did. Master always maintained a distance between himself and the other boys, mainly due to his struggle with melancholy, regrets, alcohol, and various other obsessions. That was why he was much later in seeing what the other boys had seen, what they had understood with their internal cameras. Ali and Ramazan's relationship was blossoming. They were constantly walking and sitting side by side, unable to remain still unless they were within touching distance of each other. Ramazan had immediately had Ali put into the bed next to his, banishing the child who had been sleeping there to the far end of the dormitory. Ramazan and Ali were now sleeping side by side with only a span of two hands between their beds. Then, as if this were not proof enough, there were their exuberant high spirits. Of course, Ramazan was always lively and exciting, cheerful and amusing, but the lights in his eyes sparkled when he looked at Ali, and he salivated almost uncontrollably when talking to him. Everything about Ramazan suggested a lover's insatiable desire: an insatiable desire for Ali. The Arab boy was the same. He looked at Ramazan was as if he were about to cry with happiness; he devoured him endlessly with his eyes as if he were about to die of hunger. The other children sensed it, but they were afraid of Ramazan, and they were afraid of Master. They did not have the courage to emerge from their habitual world of secrets. Consequently, they did not say anything even to each other about what was going on between Ali and Ramazan.

In the end, though, despite his mind being atrophied by alcohol, even Master cottoned on to what was happening. It was as if a sword of ice had pierced his heart when he realized the situation between Ramazan and Ali. Every movement, every breath was painful for Master. For several weeks he did not know what to do, so he resorted to more drinking. He became even more distant, wandering around the orphanage like a robot whose batteries are about to run out. Then suddenly, he had a surge of rage and acquired an energy that he had not had for years. He dashed hither and thither, shuttling back and forth from one room of the orphanage to another. If he stumbled across any children, he would hurriedly disappear into the courtyard. Then he would suddenly turn up in the study room or sniff around the dining room at mealtimes. The boys were not used to seeing Master about the place, but now they found him turning up unexpectedly at windows and doors, like an unwelcome cold draft. They started returning from school or the street at the last possible minute, trying not to be seen, their hands and feet trembling from hunger, desperate for Nezahat's disgusting gruel. Then one day, Master's randomly directed anger and energy suddenly found a target. He started to work on Ali. He targeted Ali mercilessly, tormenting him and making his life a misery. He latched on to that pure country boy, the boy who could not suppress his crying and shivering. For Ali in particular, the orphanage became a place of torture where he was a captive until the age of eighteen. Master made Ali do all the work that the cleaners neglected or could not be bothered to do. He made him clean the toilets, carry water, sweep the garden.

On some days, he kept Ali away from school and sent him off to make the boys' beds, wash their sheets and underclothes, clean the windows, polish the floors, and scrape off the layers of dirt and grease that Nezahat had been daubing over the kitchen for years. The consequence of Master's anger with Ali, and of Ali's persistence and tirelessness, was that the orphanage was transformed into a prison where it was clean enough to eat off the floor.

Of course, it was still stone cold and it still had wretched and broken furniture, but it was spotlessly clean, thanks to Ali. The orphanage staff also changed as a result of Master's torture regime. Ramazan, who hated the intolerable filth in which they had been living, was secretly almost pleased at what Ali was going through. Yes, Ali was suffering because of him. Ramazan was not stupid; he understood, he knew. But they were living in a clean place, thanks to Master venting his anger on Ali. Ramazan did feel a bit ashamed. But it was not up to him. Ali's enslavement was good for everyone else, and especially Ramazan, who was revolted by filth more than the rest of them. He accepted Ali's daily torture with a guilty happiness. Rattraps were set in various places around the orphanage to ensnare any rat that was stupid enough to come out. Master made Ali get rid of the corpses. It was the most dreadful and disgusting job at the orphanage, and the person who did this job was given the nickname "Ghoul." Master always addressed Ali by that horrid name. "Ghoul, go and hang out the washing." "Ghoul! Come here. Have you gone to sleep? Do the washing up first." "Ghoul! There's a rat in the trap. Quick march! You know what to do."

One day, Master came across a dead cat in the orphanage cellar, where the damp walls were covered with algae. Over the years, Master had taken an obsessive pleasure in lining up his rakı bottles in there. Those bottles were a summary of his life: like notches marking the futile beginning and end of every God-given day and the depth of his degradation. He painstakingly saved each and every bottle that he had downed at the orphanage with his friends. A tawny-colored cat had hidden himself away down there to await a solitary death. It was a real feral cat, with an enormous head, rotten teeth, and mangy fur—a good match for the enormous boy. "Ghoul! It's your lucky day. You've got a cat, not a rat, to throw out. You've been promoted to a higher grade of exterminator." Laughing beneath his narrow pencil-line mustache, Master sent Ali down to the cellar.

As always during these torture sessions, Ramazan averted his eyes because he did not want to see Master's face. Ali, his head bowed, went down the cellar stairs. He was a good-natured kid who always accepted whatever fate dished out to him. Ten minutes passed; then fifteen and twenty. "Ghoul! Where are you, boy? Come up here at once. Bring that dead cat up here and get rid of it!" shouted Master. There was no sound from downstairs. Ramazan became anxious, and Master's shouting was upsetting him; he dashed down to the cellar. Ali was crouched, sobbing and rocking in a corner against the rows of rakı bottles, cradling the corpse of the yellow cat, which was wrapped up like a baby in his cardigan. Ramazan fell to his knees and hugged Ali tightly. He stroked Ali's hair, murmuring, "Don't cry, Ali. Don't cry, my friend. The cat just died. He's fine; he lived and he died; his time had come."

Master became even more irate when neither Ali nor Ramazan appeared. He started to go crazy, lashing out with curses and threats, swearing on his mother's grave. Ramazan shouted back from the cellar stairs with all his might, "Fuck you and your family! Isn't it enough that I have to fuck you, asshole? Shut your bloody mouth! Say another word to Ali and I'll tear you apart! You'll be sorry you were ever born, you pimp!"

Ramazan shouted so loudly that the boys, the staff, and the whole orphanage could hear. Master's face turned beetroot red, and he flew off to his room. He would never say another word to Ali, never harass or torture him again. He would have to contain his feelings of revenge.

Master would have killed himself a thousand times rather than offend Ramazan, for whom he burned so furiously inside. He would have cut his wrists and smashed his brains in rather than live without Ramazan. Ramazan was his life. If the Arab had to be on the scene, then so be it. Just so long as Ramazan was not angry or offended. Just so long as Ramazan did not disappear from his life.

Master could not live without Ramazan. He would kill himself if Ramazan left him for good. That was for sure.

DOORMAT 6

Master had a wife and two little girls. Actually, the girls were not so little. The older one had turned twelve, just one year younger than Ramazan. The smaller girl was about five. Doormat, Master's wife, had become pregnant when they were in Maltepe. Ramazan could not remember exactly when he started calling Master's wife Doormat. But all the boys and staff, even Phantom Şener, who was afraid of his own shadow, had called the woman Doormat for years.

"Doormat turned up with her string bags looking very depressed." "Doormat is in for a beating." "Doormat was in tears when she came out of Master's room. Poor woman!" There was a sofa bed in Master's office where he slept two or three times a week, instead of going home.

Doormat and the girls saw less of Master than the boys did, because he spent his evenings partying either at the wine bar across the road or at the orphanage. If there was one thing Doormat found difficult to deal with, it was dragging herself to Master's room at the orphanage. In fact, Doormat could not really deal with anything in life. The way Master treated his wife was like someone who breaks and discards the crutches of a cripple, then maliciously watches to see whether she can get up and walk by clutching on to something or whether she falls down helplessly. Doormat was a feeble, helpless woman. Master had married her in his village somewhere in Thrace, brought her to the big city, and then, with total indifference, left her to fend for herself. He did not give a damn if his wife witnessed or heard about his farcical life that was daily descending further into a quagmire of darkness. Doormat's existence meant nothing to him, except as someone to take care of him. Master behaved so badly toward Doormat that Ramazan had surges of guilt when he thought that perhaps her nickname was the reason she had become so downtrodden. But the guilt did not last; it would overwhelm him maybe once a month, or once a year. On those rare occasions of guilt, Ramazan imagined that if only someone would strip away Doormat's outer shell, she (Doormat's real name was Nebile) would emerge as a beautiful and refined woman. Then he would want to sink into the ground with shame. She had been so young and beautiful in Maltepe! She never dolled herself up; she was not eye-catching or seductive. With her pallor, her delicacy and fragility, Ramazan had thought her worthy of being the mother of his dreams. For a while, he had even substituted Itır Esen for Türkan Şoray in the role of Orçun's mother because of Aunt Nebile! Ramazan remembered how, in those times, it had seemed plausible that Doormat could be the wife of a real orphanage director, rather than Master.

Anemic-looking Doormat, or Aunt Nebile, had two little wisps of girls. It always made Ramazan feel very bad to think that he was responsible for denying those three the chance of leading a normal family life. He would feel paralyzed with guilt. However, Ramazan finally came to recognize that he was merely a child who, despite being the son of rich parents, had been reduced to living in an orphanage (for how long, no one knew), and that the disgusting person responsible for everything, absolutely everything, was Master, who never spent a day without descending to rock bottom. He was the true excavator of the pit in which Ramazan was drowning. Ramazan no longer wasted time directing his resentment, anger, and hate at random. If Master not been such a despicable creature, his wife and daughters would have had a chance of a reasonable life, as would Ramazan. As Ramazan's belief that Master was mainly responsible for Doormat's wretchedness intensified, he inflicted increasing torment on Master. That, at least, was some comfort to him as he grew older. Doormat used to come to Master's room at the orphanage, hands and lips trembling, knees knocking, her face contorted by unhappiness and despair, her clothes in disarray, like a woman about to throw herself into an abyss. After such visits, Ramazan would screw Master in particularly humiliating ways, on and on until, with one final fuck, he would walk away leaving him just lying there. He took that bastard queen to the gates of hell! Master would cry, wail, complain, and plead; he would be totally humiliated, but not ashamed. Ramazan realized that Master never felt shame. Never! Master even took pleasure in sinking into shameful situations, especially at the hands of Ramazan. Especially in front of his friends when he was drunk. That way, Master was able to feel affinity with the lyrics of songs, able to rise to their emotions and identities. He reflected how every tragic line was a reflection of his own life, and became even more melancholic. He exulted in his immorality, using glances and words to display his love for Ramazan in an outrageously exhibitionist way in front of his friends. "Do you know anyone

worse than me, anyone more outrageous or immoral than me?"
he seemed to be saying, as if bragging that he had outdone the
most pathetic and disgusting of them. Those friends sat around
on the shabby sofas like crowned kings, never tiring of Master's
disgraceful performance. Night after night, they were fascinated
by his descent into depravity. "Master Adnan, you can do better
than that. Go for it!" Who knows how many nights a week they
sat admiring the drama, the contest in depravity. They would
egg him on with applause and flattery. None of this was spoken
about, of course. Nothing was ever said openly. On the surface,
the partygoers talked as if Master Adnan loved Ramazan like
the son he never had, as if it were due to his noble character that
Master embraced the insolence of this ungrateful, ill-mannered
child. That was their role: the chorus of hypocrites. But those
who said nothing sat every night at the table of white cheese,
melon, and spicy dishes. They were there at the center of it all.

The seasons passed, and Doormat became more wretched
as her husband's shame became more of a burden, and Ramazan
became even more determined to ruin Master. Master said nothing about the torment and humiliation directed at him. Whenever
Ramazan lashed out at him, he groaned with lust and was deliri-
ous with the happiness. He wept with joy, his cries coming from
every part of his lost, depraved soul and inner depths. If there
had been poison in Ramazan's cup, in fact, especially if there
were poison, Master would have drunk from that cup. All he
wanted was for Ramazan to act out his part in the songs.

"Bring it to me, so I may drink," sang Master, his eyes filling with tears of desire and passion. *"If there's poison in his
cup / Bring it to me, so I may drink."* Of course, there was always
a buddy there to egg him on. The voyeurism of his friends added
spice to it all. Oh Ramazan, you were the ruin of Adnan: a king

among men, a man of kings! You ignited him like a piece of firewood and reduced him to nothing. As his voice grew shriller, Master would delight his friends by becoming even more deranged. None of them sang as movingly as Adnan. In fact, not one of them could sing those songs at all. Oh the passion of those songs, damn them!

SCHOOL 7

The boys went to school in the mornings. At any rate, the "morning lot" did. The morning lot would leave the orphanage at about eight o'clock. Their school was within walking distance. The mosque courtyard opened onto the main street; from there they crossed the road, went straight on down, turned right then left and left again, and there was their school.

At twelve thirty, the morning lot would return to the orphanage. That is, of course, if they felt like it. There was nobody to check whether or not the morning lot came back from school. The midday lot went to school at one thirty and returned to the orphanage at about five thirty. They took it in turns, doing one year in the morning and the next in the afternoon.

"Beggars can't be choosers." It was one of Ramazan's favorite expressions. Whenever Ramazan heard a saying or proverb, he would pounce on it. He loved twisting them around and creating new expressions. Without thinking, he would just come out with some witticism as if he were saying, "Look at these marbles." Ramazan was hungry and eager for everything new, and he was the same with idioms and metaphors. Ali observed Ramazan with admiration and excitement when he pounced on sayings and proverbs, seizing new expressions and fixing them in his mind. Ali observed everything about Ramazan.

Ramazan was like a fairground whose existence Ali had never even heard of before. But now, Ali was right at the center of that fairground, and he could not take his gaze off it for even one second. He did not want to leave or move away. What if he missed a new gem that Ramazan came out with? What if Ramazan created a new game in the school playground? What if Ramazan thought up some new project, or "adventure" as Ramazan would say, and all the boys were there except Ali? What if he was left out, excluded?

Ali had been completely thrown when he learned that Ramazan was in the midday lot, as if a rug had been pulled from beneath his feet, as if he had fallen flat on his face. By the time Ali returned from school, it was time for Ramazan to set off. But no matter how quickly Ali ran back from school, he usually found he had missed Ramazan, who never stuck to orphanage routine anyway. Ramazan used to go out early. Sometimes he did not even turn up at study time. Ali did not acknowledge it, but there were nights when Ramazan did not sleep in his bed, the bed that was right next to his. On those nights, Ali did not sleep a wink. He kept listening for the opening and closing of doors, for sounds in the street. At the slightest noise, he would open his eyes to look over at Ramazan's empty bed, then force his eyes shut and cover his ears. Was Ramazan on his way; would he come? Ali used to lie in bed yearning to hear those light footsteps that he recognized so well. But there were some dreadful nights when Ramazan did not spend a single minute in his own bed. On those nights, however much Ali prayed and pleaded with God, Ramazan did not slip silently into his bed. Ali became depressed on those nights. He felt so tight and small inside that he would think of his mother. He thought of his village by the sea, and how he had loved playing with his friends where the river opened out into the sea. On those nights, Ali would cry silently, afraid that the other children would hear him and tease him. He felt dreadfully ashamed. But when he tried to suppress his tears, the need to cry would overwhelm him, and he would sob until the early hours. The following morning, Ali would be unable to concentrate on what the schoolteacher was saying. He had been put in the back row because of his size anyway, and however much he squinted, he could not make out what was written on the blackboard. His head would throb, and he would feel punch drunk. Finally, his head would drop and he would fall asleep, particularly in the first class of the day.

Yet Ali had an extraordinary talent for mathematics, as his teacher soon noted. He had an extraordinary memory, too. He had the marvelous ability to memorize with one glance what was written on a page or the blackboard. "Why do you keep falling asleep in class, Ali dear? You're such a good and clever boy. No one like you has ever come out of the orphanage before. Please listen to what I say. Pull yourself together." Ali wanted the ground to swallow him up when the teacher spoke to him like that, accentuating her words with her slender white finger. He used to bite his tongue and pinch his legs during class, anything to stay awake and keep sleep at bay. But it was no good. Ali was in such an awful state after those nights when Ramazan did not return to the dormitory that it was inevitable he would lose the battle to stay awake.

Despite making such a good start with their sweet-natured teacher, Ali did not manage to succeed at school life in Istanbul.

One reason was his love for Ramazan; another reason, of course, was that Master used to keep him away from school to do the cleaning. Actually there were many reasons: he had bad eyesight that was never discovered; there was nobody to care about him; nobody took the trouble to find out why he was not getting enough sleep. Many years later, Ramazan felt great remorse to think that Ali could have studied and become a proper man but had fallen behind at school because of his love for Ramazan. Ramazan felt destroyed because he had destroyed Ali. But they were still young, just children. If Ramazan had studied enough, he would have finished primary school two years earlier. However, he was still in his final year and, like all the boys, viewed their teacher, Miss Nevin, as a dried-up old maid. Miss Nevin was a strange woman, highly strung and out of step with the world; she was a caricature of a woman in her thirties. Her hair had fallen out owing to a nervous disposition so, for going to and from school, she wore a curious hat over a turban-like honey-colored wig. She understood very well that Ramazan was not interested in school, nor in her. She would never have control over that beautiful, sparkling, joking, lively boy, nor would she ever get him to do homework for her, or anything else. More and more often, when the final bell rang and all the children dispersed, Miss Nevin would keep Ramazan back in class. "Ramazan, why don't we do your homework together?" she would murmur, sidling up to him with a seductive look in her eyes. Sometimes she called him, "Ramo." She would say it in a strange nasal voice, yet Ramazan knew exactly what it meant. Ramazan knew it meant that Miss Nevin would pull him on to her knee. He knew how much she loved him to put his hand inside her blouse and squeeze her breasts. He knew what sounds she would make and how her eyes would glaze over. Miss Nevin had taught Ramazan everything, guiding him every step of the way. Ramazan had started to earn favors as a child prostitute from a very tender age. He was doing his job. Ramazan knew exactly what people wanted, but they were insatiable. It was bleeding him dry. He could not do it all the time. Not all the time. Everything for everyone.

UNION 8

Ramazan spent one more night at the wine bar across the road with Master's worthless friends. By then, these men, especially Master, made his stomach heave. When Ramazan felt sick, he ate more. And the more he ate, the sicker he felt. Every so often, he went out to throw up in the toilet. Then he rinsed out his mouth, returned to the table to eat even more, and was sick again.

Playing this crazy game of eating and vomiting was the only way he could endure sitting at their table. He was only able to put up with Master's glances, words, and caresses by playing this secret game. Ramazan's voice roughened from months of playing this vomiting game, and every so often a swelling would appear under his chin.

By continually eating, he was exacting some sort of revenge for what he had lost, but his body paid heavily for the hours of game playing that got him through the evening. Finally, it was time for the bar to close. That was the worst and most unbearable time for Ramazan.

Master tried to take Ramazan back with him to the orphanage, pleading with him to spend the night on the sofa bed in his room. He tottered about, trembling, his eyes full of tears, begging him again and again. But Ramazan did not want to. As each day passed, he had found the idea more and more unbearable. Intolerable.

"No!" he said, glaring at Master's inebriated face. He wanted to poke his finger into those glazed, bloodshot eyes. "Go home, you old drunk!"

"But, Ramazan," said Master in his squeaky voice.

"No buts. I said no, and I mean it, Master."

He had no wish to prolong the conversation. He did not want Master to make him promises that he would eventually accept, and then regret a million times over. Ramazan rushed out of the bar and across the street, causing a car to brake suddenly. The sound of brakes screeching ripped through the night; it sounded good to Ramazan, like vomiting. He kept running, across the mosque courtyard and into the orphanage. Softly, he opened the door with the key Master had given him. Before going up the stairs, he removed his shoes and carried them in his hand. This had become habitual recently. The boys knew very well when Ramazan did not return to sleep in the dormitory. Ramazan had never cared before, but somehow since Ali came, he had started to feel ashamed and uncomfortable about spending the night with Master.

Now Ramazan would climb the stairs softly, carrying the green-striped running shoes that he had made Master buy for him, and slip into bed. Ali's eyes always opened immediately when he returned, whatever time it was. "Are you back, Boss?" he would ask in that deep throaty voice that Ramazan loved so much. Ali would be half asleep, but he always asked, in a voice devoid of any sarcasm or insinuation. His genuine concern would make Ramazan feel racked with guilt.

Ramazan would realize then that Ali had not slept a wink but had been lying awake worrying about him as if it were the first time it had happened. On top of self-disgust, Ramazan would now feel shame and remorse. Ramazan was both sorry and pleased that Ali cared so much about him. "He loves me so much. He's a great kid!" Ramazan would say to himself happily.

But that night was different. Ali was obviously in a very deep sleep and did not hear the footsteps that Ramazan had tried to hide from him so many times. He heard nothing. He was gasping as he slept. Sometimes he opened his mouth because he could not inhale through his nose. It was not a peaceful sleep. Ali was struggling, troubled by whatever he was seeing in his sleep.

Ramazan undressed. He put on his tracksuit and was just about to get into bed, when Ali started panting and talking in his sleep.

"*Yemooo!*" he said, really drawing out the letter *o*. "*Yemooo, veynik? Yemoooo!*" That elongated "ooo" came from deep inside his throat. It was a language Ramazan did not know; the sounds were foreign to him. He sat on his bed, watching Ali, listening to him, as if he would be able to understand if he listened carefully enough. Ali's cries of "*Yemooo!*" did not stop. They came faster, in time with his breathing. Ali was now tossing from one side of the bed to the other, calling out again and again, "*Veynik? Yemooo, veynik?*" Ramazan could not bear to see Ali struggling. He was worried that, if the other boys woke up, he would have to tease him about it and call him Arab. He stroked Ali's hair gently.

"Ali, wake up. It's all right, man. You're OK. Look, I'm here now."

Ali opened his eyes and looked straight at Ramazan. He relaxed as he recognized Ramazan and smiled. "Are you back, Boss?"

Ramazan felt as though a stream of warm water were gushing through him. "Move over." He climbed into Ali's bed and pressed his face into the back of Ali's neck. Fellah was so clean; he smelled so good. Everything about him smelled pure and clean. The sound of Ali's heartbeat made Ramazan throb inside. He held him tight, pressing him with his body.

"But, Boss," stuttered Ali. Ramazan pushed his hand down between Ali's legs inside his tracksuit; he was as hard as a rod. Ramazan felt how big he was and inhaled deeply as he buried his face in Ali's neck. "Ali, come with me."

"Where, Boss?" asked Ali, gasping for breath.

"Shhh, don't ask! Or else these bastards will wake up."

Still half asleep and feeling very confused, Ali staggered out of bed and followed Ramazan. Ramazan opened the door to Master's room with the key he had brought with him, that room where Ali had never been before. He took Ali by the hand and led him inside. Ali was trembling violently, shaking like a leaf about to drop from a branch. It was as if Ramazan were the breeze and Ali were a leaf just waiting to be blown away.

Ramazan pulled out the sofa bed and, from memory, found the pillows, sheets, and blanket. He made the bed up with care, hoping that meanwhile Ali would relax and stop trembling. But Ali's teeth were chattering so loudly that Ramazan began to laugh nervously. "Stop it, you noisy bear. This isn't a cave here! Why are your teeth chattering like that? Look, it's only us here. I've made you a bed fit for a bride here."

He took Ali's hand, led him to the bed, and pressed his lips against Ali's. He kept on pressing until Ali's lips loosened, his body relaxed, and his trembling ceased. Ramazan held out his hand again.

"But, Boss!"

"Don't call me Boss. Think of me as your elder, your master, Caoutchouc!" he chuckled in his catlike way. Then Ramazan stopped and was silent. He looked deep into Ali's eyes as he caressed him. He kissed Ali's neck, his shoulders, and then slid downward. Ramazan wanted to devour Ali as he let out cries of pleasure. Ramazan wanted to take Ali, keep him, and never let him go.

Ali and Ramazan were united. It was the first time for both of them. Every time Ramazan recalled that beautiful dreamlike night, it reminded him that people only become united when they are in love. At any other time, it was simply screwing on the job. That night, for the first time, Ali and Ramazan spent the whole night together on Master's sofa bed. They became one. They became Ali and Ramazan, forever and ever.

PARTY TIME 9

In the morning, Ramazan hurried Ali out of Master's room, locked the door, and ran off to school. Ramazan deliberately did not fold up the sofa bed, nor did he put the bedding away in the drawer underneath. It was all intentional.

Ramazan intentionally left soiled sheets and an unmade bed in Master's room to make it absolutely and immediately obvious that he and Ali were together. If that was treachery, so be it! Had not Master hurt Ramazan in his time? Ramazan wanted to display their first night's sheets like a flag before the old queen. For Master, it would be a sickening, sweaty, semen-stained flag.

But for Ramazan, those sheets were a proclamation of love, a sign of his final escape from Master. In all his short life, he had never woken up in the morning feeling so happy and complete. Years later, when he was separated from Ali and could not believe he had nothing to remind him of Ali, not even a blue sheet from Master's sofa bed, not even a lock of Ali's hair, he would say, "If only we'd kept those sheets."

When Ramazan pushed Ali out of the room and dashed off to school like some eager student, Ali ran into the place that served as a bathroom. It was not the day for bathing, but the days when water was heated up for the boys to splash over themselves were so rare at the orphanage that Ali always used an old plastic jug to pour freezing-cold water over himself, because he was fastidious about cleanliness.

He did the same thing then. He was shivering, but not only because of the cold water. He could not believe what was happening to him. He was crying and feeling passionate desire for Ramazan at the same time. He missed Ramazan. If only Ramazan were there and they could be united again and again. That was what Ali craved.

The shivering did not stop at school, neither the shivering nor the tears. They just would not stop. When lessons were over, the teacher took Ali by the hand and sat him opposite her at an empty desk. "What is it, Ali dear? You look terrible today. Has something happened? Is something happening at the orphanage to upset you?"

"No, no, m-miss. I-I'm f-fine, thank you," stammered Ali. He was very scared that his dear teacher would realize what had happened. He wanted to shout out, "I'm so happy, miss. It's the first time I've been so happy since my mother died!"

Master intercepted Ramazan when he finally returned exhausted to the orphanage as night fell, having won all the marbles between Fatih and Aksaray. "Ramazan?" He looked straight at Ramazan with eyes swollen from crying. Master seemed to think he only had to utter Ramazan's name and Ramazan would explain, apologize, wink, and say, "Don't worry about it, Master." Ramazan realized immediately that, however ridiculous, this was what Master was hoping for.

"What is it? Has something happened?" asked Ramazan.

"You're coming for dinner tonight, aren't you?" asked Doormat's husband as usual. However, this time Master was torn with anxiety and embarrassment, yet still he hoped and begged.

"At the wine bar?" shouted Ramazan so that the other boys and the staff would understand how vile Master was. He wanted to humiliate Master, crush him, send him to rock bottom!

"You know what I mean," said Master, pleading with swollen eyes. He put out his tongue and licked the thin pencil-line mustache on his upper lip.

"Snake!" thought Ramazan. "That snake hasn't learned his lesson yet. Look at that long tongue, just like a snake." "Fine," he said, "I'll come along with Ali."

"With Ali? How did Ali come on the scene?"

"He probably came out of his mother's belly. I'm not coming unless I come with him, Master."

"OK, come together then," sighed Master.

"Just listen to the creep!" thought Ramazan with delight. "He whines like a dog!" That night in the wine bar, Ramazan and Ali sat opposite Master's contemptible friends, their thighs touching all the time. Whenever Ramazan managed to catch Ali's hand, he squeezed it tightly under the table. Ali's hands were trembling; so were his feet. Ramazan was upset that Ali felt so ashamed and embarrassed, but he loved him even more. He had never encountered such a pure, innocent person in his life before.

Master resorted to singing the lines of a song in front of his boisterous friends. *"I'm the sorrow of fall, you're the joy of spring,"* he sang in his high-pitched, manic voice. Master made Ramazan sit next to him, yet he realized that Ramazan had time only for Ali and that the two boys could not stop rubbing their legs against each other. Master seemed to think that if he brought all his shameful force to bear, Ramazan would lurch his way, as if on a seesaw, and be his alone. Master reached out, took hold of Ramazan's head, and turned it toward him; he tried to enslave Ramazan with his eyes as he sang to the doleful sounds of the Turkish art music. When the song reached the lines "*You are the melody in my heart / Oh sweetness of love, flame of passion,*" Master's voice became even more brittle in his delirium. He grabbed Ramazan's other hand from under the table and raised it to his lips. Master kissed Ramazan's fingers and the palm of his hand, then rocked back and forth seeking relief in his glass as he continued to massacre the song with his crying.

"Cut it out!" thought Ramazan. He could not stand seeing Master behaving like a crazed actor in a one-man play. Instead of calming him down, Ramazan pulled his hand away and, holding on to Ali, lashed out at Master.

"Enough, for God's sake! If you're the Master, act like one! Get the fuck out of my life. I'm thirteen years old—can't you see that, you son of a bitch! Pimp!"

Everyone in the wine bar froze as if someone had pressed an invisible stop button. They all abandoned their ribaldry and turned to look.

"Shame on him!" shouted someone like a shrewish old woman. "The ungrateful dog has no shame! Is that any way to talk to Master Adnan, head of the great orphanage? Queers! Look at them, everything about them says they're queers. They may be kids, but they've already screwed each other!"

Ramazan's eyes darkened with anger and rage. Quick as lightning, with superhuman speed, he landed a blow on Master's face, then two more, a left and a right. Ramazan grabbed hold of Ali and they flung themselves out of the wine bar.

When they reached the door of the orphanage, Ali stared at Ramazan with a bewildered, sorrowful look and said, "He called us queers, Boss. Are we queers? Have I become a queer?" "Shhhh," said Ramazan. "Don't use that word. We're not queer or anything, we're lovers. OK? We're just in love." He covered Ali's lips with kisses; Ali's head began to spin with happiness. For Ali, nothing apart from Ramazan would be important ever again. Never. Ali had understood it the moment their bodies were united. Deep inside, he knew that he had become locked in with Ramazan. Ramazan was his life, and he had become Ramazan's life. He felt it in his bones. Ali ached for Ramazan.

II

YEARS 10

Ramazan did not believe that the next six or seven years could fly by so fast. He realized that they were good years that were full of happy and pleasant times, but could not understand how they passed so quickly. But later he would understand. When they had to endure those terrible years, when time was divided into endless suffocating, heartbreaking hours and minutes, when every moment tore him apart and broke his spirit—then he would understand.

Master finally had to curtail his nights in the wine bar opposite the orphanage, that bar where he was such a respected customer that he could sit a thirteen-year-old boy in the window until closing time. Master obtained a sick note from Haseki Hospital and shut himself away at home. He disappeared to drink himself into a stupor under the protection of Doormat. For Master, without Ramazan, without the nights they spent together on the sofa bed, without being able to look into Ramazan's eyes and caress him as he crooned those lovely songs, life was so empty that he spent months trying to drink himself to death. But death did not come. However, eventually, Master managed to physically disable himself by having a stroke that left the whole of his right side paralyzed.

Master was almost relieved that it was no longer possible to get Ramazan back. He took early retirement and went to live in his village in Thrace with Doormat and his daughters. During his final years with Doormat, Master attained some inner peace, in the knowledge that he was now spared the torture of secretly hoping and waiting, and was freed from the fear of retribution for what he had been doing all those years.

Ramazan heard Master's voice one last time when Phantom Şener held out the phone to him. Master sounded like a sick old man, gasping for breath as his words rolled unintelligibly around in his mouth! Ramazan was delighted to hear that broken voice, the voice of a man who would be an invalid for the rest of his life. It soothed him inside a little, but that was all.

Later, Ramazan forgot about Master. Or so he thought. Master's invalid condition was what he deserved; Master's complete removal from their lives meant revenge had been exacted. For Ramazan, Master had been discarded and wiped from his memory. Yet for years, many years, Ramazan would have dreams about fighting off Master. Innumerable times, Ramazan would kill him in the most bloody and violent manner. He would yell and shout, hurling insults to his face until his breathing stopped. Innumerable times, Ramazan would wake, dripping with sweat, from a sleep of hate.

However, because Master was no longer in their lives, the nightmares disappeared when he awoke. What can one do about someone who is not visible, or who is only visible in dreams? Master was dead, finished, gone. It was as though he had never existed, never even been born. Phantom Şener became the orphanage director. Surprisingly, he actually did a worthwhile job. He was certainly much better than Master!

Of course, that was not such a difficult thing to achieve, given Master's nihilistic attitude, his feebleness, and his lack of interest in anything other than the tragic decline of his obsessive love.

Peace and order now descended over the orphanage. Miss Nezahat was persuaded to retire and replaced by an obsessively clean young woman from the Black Sea region. The meals were not wonderful; while some of the local dishes were edible, they were still difficult to swallow. But the kitchen was spotlessly clean. So was the dining room and everywhere else. The cleaners started to truly work. The tutors pulled themselves together and actually did their jobs. There were two anonymous members of staff whose functions the boys never knew. These men were replaced every two years, but at least they now sat at their desks and were always busy writing something or other. At Director Şener's request, the magnanimous State started sending a psychologist to the orphanage three times a week. Miss Nurşin tripped into the building in her high-heeled shoes and tight skirt, with a little makeup on her lovely face, to spend three hours or so attending to the boys' needs and achieving nothing. Nothing was achieved because the boys had been scarred from a tender age. The lady psychologist was unable to do anything about their deprivation or the fact that they were trapped in the orphanage. First and foremost, they could never forget that the moment the giant invisible clock chimed the hour heralding their eighteenth birthday, they would be turned out of the building, whatever their circumstances!

Miss Nurşin (that's how they addressed her; they were not comfortable calling her Doctor Nurşin) spent most of her time with Ali. She liked working with him, partly because Ali wanted it, and partly because he was the most sensitive, damaged, and good-natured of all the boys.

The boys started washing at least once a week on a regular basis. The sheets were changed every week, their clothes were washed, and outgrown clothes were replaced. No longer did they walk around in outgrown clothes that were too short, too tight, or ripped and stained in a way that trumpeted their existence as ORPHANAGE CHILDREN from a mile away! Of course, Ramazan had never walked around like that. However, he still felt uncomfortable, even now that they were able to obtain fresh clothes, fill their bellies, and have the occasional wash. The discomfort and shame that he felt inside gradually passed as the effects of the way they had been forced to live began to fade. In any case, Ramazan had always been used to dressing better than the other boys, to leading a better life and being different, superior. This habit of seeing himself as better than the other boys helped to soften the memories that were frozen into his mind. When the chance arose, he started selling himself at beer houses in Aksaray and in the parks around Sultanahmet, which were very close to the orphanage and just right for that sort of thing. On the nights that Ramazan returned late to the orphanage or did not return at all, Ali was still unable to sleep until morning because he thought Ramazan was up to something. If he did sleep, it was even worse, because his sleep was troubled and broken. Nevertheless, for better or worse, they struck up some sort of balance. Ramazan gauged the intervals between his outings well, and Ali kept a check on the intensity of his sorrow and jealousy.

After those two boys had been plucked out of the orphanage, tossed about and left to stumble through life, only to pick themselves up and stumble again, Ramazan would realize that he had received the best and most humane treatment of his life during those six or seven years at the orphanage. They would always miss those days at the orphanage: the peace that Phantom Şener brought to the place, the comfort of knowing they had a bed to sleep in and food to eat—like dogs. At the top of the list of bad things that were to happen in the lives of Ali and Ramazan was military service. Phantom Şener was very decent toward Ramazan. He ignored the fact that, since Ramazan was a year older than Ali, he was not supposed to stay at the orphanage, or sleep there, while waiting to be drafted into the army. Ramazan was working in a sweatshop near the orphanage and counting the days in fear. Before long, he would be separated from Ali, and all his connections with the orphanage would be severed. He would have to face the fact that he was a nobody with no identity, with nothing. There would be days when he could not even conjure up the Turkish Film Kid. When the conscription papers arrived, all those fears, expectations, and realities poured over him like boiling water. Ramazan was conscripted for a year and a half to serve in the Glorious Army of the Fatherland.

MILITARY SERVICE

Ramazan's military service passed in a tangle of unease, point-lessness, and apprehension. After completing the basic training, it was decided that, because he was a beautiful youth, Ramazan should remain in Istanbul. He spent his military service as a waiter at Sarıyer Barracks.

It was a breeze, but Ramazan had become so used to being presented with the sweet things of life one way or another that he failed to recognize what a stroke of luck this was. He also failed to appreciate all the benefits of training to be a waiter in that enormous edifice overlooking the sea, or the ease and comfort in which he was doing his military service. The spoiled, crazy boy failed to see how the nation's children suffered in order to pay their debt to the country, how some were left crippled and others only returned to their villages for their own funerals. Ramazan had no idea why military service was compulsory. Even though he had been raised by the State in an orphanage, he could not for the life of him understand why he was in debt to the nation, Goddamn it.

"How can I be in debt when nothing's ever been done for me? What's the nation got to do with me? If I had any debts, I've paid them back in my own way, on the streets."

"Shut up, Ramazan. Someone will hear you, and you'll get into trouble. It's just what people say. It's not that we have debts; we just have to go and do it, that's all. Anyway, you're learning to be a waiter. What more do you want?"

Ramazan had turned up at the orphanage on his first day of leave, and Ali was trying to calm him down. He was always afraid that Ramazan would get into trouble and be locked up for speaking out like this. Ali also feared that when it was his turn, they would be posted to opposite ends of the country and would not see each other for weeks or months at a time. What would happen to them then?

Ramazan just had to get through his military service without knowing what these debts and benefits were (certainly no benefit had come his way). He felt trapped and straightjacketed by having to conform to pointless regulations. In the first place, he was irritated by the way his hair was cut so short and by the ridiculously tight little white jacket and black trousers that constituted the uniform of an army waiter. Everything irritated him, but Ramazan had no right to make any comment. If he did, what would happen? The State would come down on him even more heavily. Hang him out to dry. Extend his conscription.

Was that not what the State always did to Ramazan anyway? Whatever deprivation, harm, or pain he had been subjected to during his days with Master, Ramazan was still supposed to be grateful to the State. Why? Because he had been looked after at the orphanage. And now he was supposed to feel grateful that he was about to spend eighteen months doing a cushy military service. As time passed, all the pointlessness, hypocrisy, and pretense irritated Ramazan even more. He was also greatly distressed to see how Ali was dreading his own conscription; without Ramazan, he would probably go to pieces.

The sweatshop where Ramazan had worked suddenly closed. Actually, the closure was not so sudden; business had not been good, and the owner could not raise any more credit. This meant that Ali and the other boys were now out of a job. At first it was reassuring to think that Ramazan was employed, even if it was in the army, but the realization that he would develop friendships with other boys kicked off a completely new, monstrous fear that was unlike anything Ali had known before. What if Ramazan went off with one of them while he was in the army and Ali was waiting? It was only thanks to Şener that Ali was able to remain at the orphanage, but that was just until he went into the army. Ali had no work, no connections, no family, no money. He could tolerate anything, resign himself to anything, but Ramazan was starting to slip away from him. Starting? Or had Ramazan gone already? Was it over?

What was left for Ali? What was left in life? Ali started taking solvents. And in no half measures! Ramazan immediately understood what was happening. "Caoutchouc!" he shouted at Ali. "I'm bored and fed up there. But it's not enough for you that I'm having a bad time. Now you've turned into a huffer. That's all I need. Screw you, man!" Ali's eyes stared at the floor. But his need for solvents was so great he could not believe why he had not started on them before. He no longer felt the heat or cold. But most importantly, he did not feel lonely; he did not miss Ramazan or his mother. For the first time in Ali's life, he did not miss his mother. The solvents seemed to coat his soul with plastic. It was as if his heart were cushioned by a bubble of transparent plastic. Nothing and nobody, no sorrows or worries could touch Ali. That was how the solvents made him feel. The solvents protected him. Ali's soul no longer burned, either inside or outside, when he inhaled solvents. His spirit was not on fire. He felt no distress, no sensation that he was sinking or suffocating. If he was suffocating, it was from the solvents. Never mind. It was still good. Apart from Ramazan, had anything been so good to Ali as solvents?

Ramazan's time in the army was a kind of hell in which he worried about Ali, about their future, or lack of it; he even worried about his worries. One and a half years taken away, just like that. The State was taking revenge on everyone—for nothing. Was this not the same State that had produced Master, his bugbear since he was just a pint-sized child? Ramazan almost breathed a sigh of relief when Ali was taken into the army four months before his own discharge. At least the Arab bear would get away from solvents and come to his senses. Just as long as he was not posted anywhere dangerous or sent out to fight in the east of the country. As long as he did not return in a body bag.

Ali drew Çanakkale as his posting. "The domain of martyrs is a good place to spend your military service," said Ramazan to Ali on the telephone, chuckling like a cat. That chuckle was the worst thing about Ramazan.

"You'll miss me, Ramazan, won't you?" Ali asked in a tearful voice. His head was clear of solvents now; it was his own voice speaking, not the voice of solvents. It was the deep, throaty voice that Ramazan loved. All the worries, fears, and anxieties about solvents that Ramazan had been harboring just disappeared. They melted away, taking with them any residue of doubt.

"Who else would I miss, Caoutchouc?" said Ramazan. "Who else do I have? Has there ever been anyone else?"

"Never. There hasn't, has there, Ramazan? You're all I have, and I..." gulped Ali, unable to complete his sentence.

"Hey! The Turkish cinema duo! Don't do a Hülya Koçyiğit on me, Jungle-boy. The audience will think you're Tarzan's gorilla."

To Ali, the sound of Ramazan laughing was like pure water running through his insides. It warmed him. Thank God for Ramazan. Oh Ramazan! "The line's very long, I'd better go now. It's not fair on the others; they're getting impatient, Ramazan."

Ali could not say, "I love you." He was never able to say it and never would be able to. Never. Such talk embarrassed him.

Ramazan finished his military service, but when he returned to the Fatih-Aksaray-Sultanahmet district, there was nobody left at the orphanage to smuggle him inside for the night. He hid at the back of the mosque courtyard. He could no longer worm his way into the illustrious orphanage carved out of a madrasa, because it had closed down. Koran courses were held there now. In Bakırköy, a gigantic brand-new children's home was being built: Bakırköy Children's Home. Having returned home after paying off whatever debt to the State he was supposed to have had, Ramazan cursed vividly that there was no roof, canvas, or even hollow where he could take shelter. He was just a foul-mouthed boy. What should the State do with the likes of him? Fill his mouth with chili pepper? Beat him? Put him down a hole? Things were the way they were, and they were to go on that way.

BEATING 12

Ramazan's return to Istanbul made his previous life, both at the orphanage and in the army, seem easy. "We had it all and didn't know it!" The Istanbul winter was starting just as Ramazan was about to begin his new life as a nobody among the poor of Istanbul. "Why did it have to be fucking winter? How unlucky is that. Being an orphanage kid was better than this."

Once they were eighteen, the State turned thirty-three boys out of Mevlanakapı Hostel to take shelter in the Surlar area next to Istanbul's historic city walls. There they lived, or rather hung on to life, like cave boys struggling to survive. At nighttime, they burned brushwood and rolls of newspaper inside barrels stolen from Tahtakale. They put anything they could find inside those barrels, sprinkled it all with spirits, and set it alight. Their hands only got warm if they held them right over the fire. Yet while their hands were on the point of burning, they barely felt any heat at all inside. Their feet might as well have been completely detached from their bodies. No matter how hot their hands became, something seemed to prevent any heat reaching their feet.

Whatever Ramazan did, his feet remained like blocks of ice. The best solution was to wear several layers of newspaper around their socks; but then their feet would not fit into their shoes, so the boys stood in front of the fire in rubber slippers. The best ones for that were the ugly slippers they found on garbage dumps. Their feet looked like elephant feet with all the newspapers bound around them. "My fucking feet. If only they'd warm up and stop gnawing at my insides; if only I could stop thinking about them!" Sometimes, Ramazan just wanted to be able to cut off his feet. He wanted to do the same to his hands, because they could not send heat down to his feet quickly enough and because they were chapped and painful. At times, he wanted to cut off his hands and feet, curl up into a ball, and go to sleep next to the burning barrel. While Ramazan was struggling to survive the cold, hunger, and deprivation along with the other kids at Surlar, what he missed more than anything was somewhere warm to sleep. He yearned for a safe place where he could have an uninterrupted sleep. "Everything I own has holes in it! I'm all holes, Goddamn it. I've turned into Colander Ramazan. There's nowhere left of me that isn't full of holes." He tried to do his catlike chuckle, but did not manage it.

Every day, Ramazan was becoming more like a hyena from the hunger, cold, and sleeplessness. His increasing resentment against life began to earn him a reputation around Surlar. Every so often, families from nearby houses, not those actually on the walls but the houses that overlooked the area where the boys were camping at Surlar, felt obliged to send their menfolk over to tell the boys to clear off.

One night, three or four guys from a delegation of cowardly bullies suddenly appeared a short distance away. "Boy, get your junk together and clear off! You'll end up starting a fire or something. This is a place of historic significance, and you're making the families here uneasy. We're telling you to get out of here, do you understand, boy?"

"What harm are we doing you, mister? If we had somewhere to go, do you think we'd stick around in this shithole?"

"Who do you think you are, you son of a bitch!" said Aranan, the fiercest of the men. He looked as if he were going to set upon the boys, as if he thought Ramazan were insulting his own family when he cursed the Surlar district.

"Listen to him. The words of an artist!" said Ramazan. "Anyone would think Surlar belonged to your father." The other men rushed in and, grabbing his arms, dragged Aranan away. Aranan swaggered, as if he had been on the verge of getting into a skirmish with the boys and smashing Ramazan's face in. As if.

"Hold on to the stupid moron. See he doesn't get away," shouted Ramazan aggressively. He had guessed correctly that Aranan's aggression was all bluster, that Aranan confidently expected his friends to hold him back, and that he would never have had the courage to get into a fight with the youths.

"Son of a bitch! I'll smash your face in!" shouted Aranan, the veins on his neck bulging. As he shouted, the delegation of fathers gradually pulled him away.

"Clear off, asshole! Does Surlar belong to you?" yelled Ramazan. He was now in his element, and to cap it all, the man was actually backing down. He spat on his right fist and punched the palm of his left hand.

Aranan was still raving, but was successfully dragged away by the other fathers. Eventually, they all returned to the comfort of evening family life. Within an hour, a fleet of vehicles had parked down below. Three policemen, two uniformed and one plainclothes, got out of one car and start climbing up toward Surlar.

"Shit, we've had it now!" cried Recep. Policemen meant bad news in that part of the world. It was a sign of bad things to come. It meant you were fucked.

"What are you doing around here? You're scaring the families. This isn't a shelter for stray dogs. This is the Republic of Turkey!" shouted the plainclothes policeman obnoxiously. This policeman had a strangely shaped mustache that curled down both sides of his lips. He glared with glassy, ice-cold blue eyes. They were not like human eyes, but looked as if they had been manufactured and stuck into his eye sockets.

"Mister, we're not doing anything, really we're not. We're just hanging around here," said Ramazan in his most charming voice.

"Is it you who's been threatening the men around here and getting into fights? You son of a bitch. Who the hell do you think you are?" He hit Ramazan with the back of his hand so hard that Ramazan saw stars, just as they do in comic strips.

"I said we didn't do anything." Ramazan stopped himself from adding "man," but his voice sounded loud and insolent.

The policeman with the icy glare and odd mustache was enraged by this youth. He did not understand how the boy could answer back like that, and he became abnormally irritated. Quite abnormally! "Come here, boy!" he said, grabbing hold of Ramazan's collar. "Is this what you want, huh?" he said repeatedly, as he hit him over and over again.

Ramazan lay spread-eagle on the ground, and the policeman started kicking his face. The other policemen started to become uneasy. Blue-eyes looked as though he was going to go too far. Taking hold of his arms, the other policemen said something quietly to Blue-eyes and bundled him into the police car. Then they turned around and marched Ramazan and three randomly selected boys off to the police station.

"People have made complaints about you." At the police station they kept repeating this, like parrots. "You're worrying the families."

Ramazan looked like a sack of meat and bones after his beating. He slithered off his chair and collapsed onto the floor. The policemen paced around him. There was one nice young policeman, and there is always one, who brought Ramazan a glass of water. He sat Ramazan down on the floor with his back against the wall and put a blanket over him. Ramazan's face was swollen, split open, and covered with heavy bruising. For the first time in his life, he was no longer beautiful. He trembled violently from the cold, the blows, and the pain.

Blue-eyes was very angry with the young policeman for being kind to Ramazan. "That's not how we do it in the police," he said, putting his cigarette on Ramazan's neck. He pressed hard, stubbing out the cigarette on the back of Ramazan's neck. Ramazan gritted his teeth until, eventually, when he was at the point of losing his mind from the pain, he let out such a scream that the chief inspector came rushing in.

"What's going on here, boys? What's happened?"

The nice young policeman, feeling guilty and unhappy that somehow he was responsible for this last act of cruelty, spoke up saying, "He beat him up, sir, and now he's stubbed out his cigarette on the boy's neck, sir." He was a clean, upright Anatolian boy who had not become a policeman to see unfortunates treated in that way. His eyes filled with tears, and he felt ashamed at this outrageous behavior.

The chief inspector sent Ramazan to stay at Adli Tıp Hospital for a few days to get a medical report, and he made a complaint against the mustachioed Blue-eyes. The man had gone too far! There was an accepted way of carrying out police beatings, and excess was not tolerated. The State's golden rule for achieving manhood was that, if you escaped a beating in the army, you got one from the police or vice versa. If you were unlucky enough to have both, so much the better!

Ramazan, having cruised through his military service, finally realized this from his beating by a lowdown Turkish policeman. Ramazan spent three days in the hospital, during which he swore he would never again sink so low. No policeman, family man, or passerby would ever disgrace him like that again. When he left the hospital, he kept his vow and made a beeline for the prostitution racket. He plunged into male prostitution with great determination and with pleasure. The Aksaray neighborhood was the best place for pulling, and very soon Ramazan became the best-known gigolo in the area.

Well, what else would you expect? He had spent his childhood in an orphanage. That, of course, was an advantage.

LONELINESS 13

The first resolution Ramazan made after the beating was that he would not stick around with the other boys anymore. They were no longer at the orphanage, and they did not even have the protection of a tumbledown bit of an old madrasa, so what was the point of sticking with the other orphanage boys?

"You're not even an orphan anymore," he thought, as he realized just how utterly insignificant he was. "You'll get nowhere by sticking with them!" he kept repeating to himself as a sort of mantra. He kept repeating it in order to resist being drawn back to them like mercury. But they were like brothers to him. He had grown up with them, and they all spoke the same language, the orphanage language, a special tongue of orphans. However, to tread the downward slope with them, to be a traveler on the never-ending road to the bottom—no, that was not what Ramazan wanted! After his beating, a new Ramazan was born. So what if he was a prostitute! But he was not the son of a prostitute. That was very important to Ramazan, who still believed his mother to be an angel, a chaste and virtuous woman in a world of bastards.

Ramazan's mother was now none other than Türkan Şoray of Yücel Çakmaklı Films. In her white muslin headscarf, Türkan Şoray was continually crying for Ramazan, praying for the beautiful baby she had been forced to abandon in a mosque courtyard. Ramazan was renting out his body as a paid gigolo. Call it whatever you want, labels change nothing. "The world can't manage without prostitutes, and I've become a prostitute, so what? But I'm not the son of a prostitute. I'm not like the rest of them." Ramazan would console himself in this way. He needed to keep this thought coursing through his brain.

He was now alone, totally alone. Like a dog, a mangy stray dog! He discovered a cinema called the Ace Cinema. After midnight, he frequently went there and slept on the doormat, all alone in a space sheltered by glass on two sides. Sometimes, he slept in Sirkeci or Haydarpaşa Station, but his favorite sleeping spot was the Ace Cinema. It was more luxurious, more sheltered, and he could be sure of sleeping alone. There were always other down-and-outs at the stations, which he found depressing. He wanted no reminder of what he had become. If he could just be alone. If he was living the life of a street dog, so what? He might be a rich kid having a go at being homeless for a while. No, that was going too far. He was in fact living like a street dog. Nobody was going to come and save him. If he was ever to be saved, he would have to save himself. Ever since the beating, loneliness was part of his wretchedness.

Ramazan found work in Taksim, where he chose his clients, like picking hairs out of butter. Then he would take them to the places he knew best, mostly in Aksaray and Sultanahmet. He screwed in graveyards and parks. Sometimes it was Sirkeci, sometimes Tarlabaşı—in seedy hotels, saunas, hamams, and cars. Occasionally, if really pressed and the client was prepared to pay top rates, he went to their houses. However, Ramazan did not like going to men's houses. Most of them were married; a few still lived with their parents. These family men were able to take Ramazan back to their homes because their folk had been packed off somewhere, or had gone to visit relatives. But their houses smelled of women and children. To Ramazan, all those houses smelled of Doormat and her daughters. Ramazan found it unbearable. The discomfort, guilt, and shame, which in childhood he had not fully recognized, came flooding back, bringing memories of Master's sofa bed. He did not like houses that smelled of women and children, especially babies. On one occasion, a client forced Ramazan to go with him to his house where a baby buggy was standing at the entrance. His wife was at the market with her mother and baby! The man wanted to get down to business straight away. He was so excited that his face was bright red as he gave orders to Ramazan. "Come on, my young lion. Come on, my ram! Come on! Come on!" A baby's feeding bottle was lying on the kitchen table. Ramazan could not help picking it up while the man went off to get dressed. It was still warm. Ramazan suddenly felt queasy at the thought that he had screwed the father of a baby who would shortly return from market with its mother. Ramazan was disgusted with the man and also with himself. Opening a drawer, he took out a large knife and pressed it against the man's throat when he came back into the kitchen. "Give me double rate. You didn't tell me you had a kid, you son of a bitch!" The family man handed over double money without a murmur and then tried to arrange a rendezvous for the same time the following week. Ramazan managed to get away from him and out into the street. "The son of a bitch actually liked me holding a knife to his throat. He was excited that his wife might arrive back from the market and discover us. It gave him a real turn-on. He was squawking like a cockerel with a slit throat. Bastard! His poor baby and wife!" He continued to screw the man and pocket the money.

Then, just when the weather was improving, just when it was becoming easier to find a place to sleep and get through the night, his homelessness hit him. Loneliness also got to him. Ramazan was missing Ali more than he could ever have imagined with all the screwing going on. Ramazan realized that dreaming about Ali was the one thing he had to hold on to in his life as a gigolo. Ali was Ramazan's only chance of decency, his only link with transparency, beauty, and goodness. Even when up to his neck in shit, Ramazan was able to keep a vision of Ali in his mind, to dream of his love for Ali and of Ali's love for him. He was able to imagine that he was still clean and could remain so.

"You're the only decent thing in my life, Ali," he said on the telephone one Saturday. It was the first time Ali had heard such words from Ramazan. He felt numb with happiness; his legs seemed to be giving way, and he had to sit down. "Not much longer, Ramazan," he said, not knowing how to reply. "Four months, three weeks, and five days left."

"How the hell have you memorized your discharge date, you Arab bear!" said Ramazan, reverting to his usual blasé indifference, his old droll, wisecracking self. But he could not believe what he had admitted to Ali. Yet it was true. Ramazan was not sure he could survive his sordid life without Ali; he was not sure at all. "Aliiii," he would howl some nights. After all that sex, all that filth, after that filthy sex, Ramazan wanted to cleanse himself by making love to Ali.

Shortly before Ali's return, Ramazan, who had tired of hotel rooms, took a room on the ground floor of a rundown building in Mirialem Street, Fındıkzade. "Ali will sort it out," thought

Ramazan. "He'll clean it up and make it like home. Ali, you cleanse me. Come and wash me, inside and out." His heart ached, and his eyes filled with tears of longing. As Ali's return grew closer, Ramazan was missing him so much that for three weeks he did not go with anybody. He could not make himself do it. Ramazan got hold of a few basic essentials for the apartment. He bought a small refrigerator, a folding table and two chairs, a pillow for Ali, and a double mattress. Then he sat staring at the blank walls, waiting for Ali. During those days of waiting, Ramazan recognized what Ali had known from the start. He understood that alone he was nothing, but as Ali and Ramazan, they were complete, they meant something. Ramazan's respect for Ali grew while he stared at the blank walls waiting for Ali. By the time Ali was due to return, Ramazan had spent so long lying on the mattress and crying for Ali that he felt internally cleansed from top to toe. "Ali, I washed myself inside and out with tears before you came, man. I'm like a newborn babe, Caveboy. Ooh, how I love you!" said Ramazan, covering Ali's neck with kisses when he met him at the station. Ali blushed deeply with embarrassment, worried that people would take it the wrong way. They were lovers, not queers. They were both male. Fine, so what if they were lovers? Of what concern was it to anyone else?

TOGETHER 14

Ramazan would never forget their first days and nights in Mirialem Street.

For four or five days after Ali returned from military service, Ramazan showered him with love in their shoebox of a room, hoping to ward off any subsequent complications or pain in their relationship. He wanted to believe in the possibility that Ali, and they as a couple, would get better and not feel suffocated, withdraw, and drift apart.

Ali returned from the army an extremely handsome and fit young man. He seemed even taller, slimmer, and stronger, and his skin had turned a deep brown from being in the open air. Ali came back with no trace of solvents, pills, or alcohol in his system. "Wow, look at you," Ramazan kept saying to his lover. "The Turkish Army's made a real man of you!"

"They wanted to make me a sergeant," said Ali, showing his even, white teeth. "They were really pleased with me. They said I'm just the type they're looking for."

"And you're just what I'm looking for! Never mind the Turkish Army." Ramazan had filled the place with Ali's favorite food. Meatballs, pilafs, bulgur salads, spicy pastries, cos lettuces, mature kaşar cheese, pastırma. He went round all the meze sellers in Mısır Market buying food for his lover. He bought rakı, beer, and bags of ice, which he put in the refrigerator, and even a bucket to put the ice in. During the last couple of days, Ramazan had thought of everything and anything that might please Ali. He bought milky desserts, grapes, walnuts, figs, and roasted chickpeas. He filled up the place to such an extent that Ali was lost for words when he arrived. Ali just stood there in the middle of their little room, his eyes filling with tears. He was frozen to the spot, and his beautiful dark, coffee-colored eyes that had cried so much for Ramazan were now brimming with tears again.

"Is this all for me, Ramazan? You went and bought all this for me?"

"Well, you're the handsomest bear cub I know! I've missed you so much, Ali. I couldn't help myself." Ramazan pulled Ali toward him. More than anything, he had missed Ali's mouth. He had missed kissing him, inhaling his pure breath and feeling his tongue. Ramazan never kissed the men he screwed unless he had to. He did not want to open his heart to them, nor show them his entire body. He only let them have what they paid for, nothing more. Anything more belonged to Ali, Ramazan's Ali. Within a few moments, they fell onto the mattress, attacking each other like wild wolves. Ramazan had an overwhelming desire to caress and feel, suck and bite Ali's flawless brown skin. For days, they ate meze, dried fruits, and nuts, and made love. For days, the only time they left the room was to go to the toilet on the floor below. When they tired, they collapsed and slept a little, until they woke and started attacking each other all over again, as if they were hungry for meat, for each other's meat. The more they had of each other, the greater the hunger with which they came back for more. Their appetite for each other was insatiable. Finally, their bodies and souls were exhausted from making love and from loving. And there was not a morsel of food left to eat. Even the ice had melted away. Actually, Ramazan was scared of taking a step outside. He knew he would find no work. Even if he did, it would be at the lowest possible rates, and he would be forced to return to screwing men as his only option.

"The water jug always breaks on the way to the well." Ramazan tried to prepare Ali for their future with clichés like this. "We've got this far, Jungle-boy. As you know, Ramazan never looks back." He did his cat chuckle. Ali knew that Ramazan's cat chuckle signified that everything was about to turn bad. He was frightened by this chuckle.

"Don't chuckle like that, Ramazan. You don't have to do it! Not with me anyway. It makes me nervous."

"What's the matter, old Caoutchouc! Has your tire punctured? I'm just getting you prepared. You know what I do for a living, don't you, Ali?"

Ali walked out, banging the door. He knew all too well that they had reached the end of Ramazan's preparation stage, but as long as he lived, he would never be as laid back as Ramazan. He might know what Ramazan's work was, but he could not acknowledge it. He could not openly put it into words.

When Ali returned home, he found Ramazan had drunk all the beer and rakı he could find. "I'll work, Ramazan. Please, give me more time to look for work," pleaded Ali. "But don't force me into anything. I'll find a job and look after both of us. I promise you, I'll take care of you. I'll do anything. Just a bit more time."

"Yeah, yeah. There are thousands of jobs out there. Our friends from the sweatshop are waiting for you. They live like rats out at Surlar, looking for work, night and day. Who the hell's going to give us a job? You might as well stick your primary school diploma up your ass. It's no good for anything else."

"Shut up! For God's sake, hold your tongue!" shouted Ali in a way that startled Ramazan.

"Take it easy," said Ramazan with a grin. However, he said no more. It was not easy coming back to reality after five days and all those hours of lovemaking. Ramazan went to the bathroom for a good long wash. The cold water sobered him up and brought him to his senses; it also gave him a chance to analyze their situation.

He returned to the room and dressed. Ali realized then that there was no stopping Ramazan. Ali understood, but what could he do? Ramazan went out to work, and Ali dashed out to the nearest hardware store. Without paint thinner to dull his senses, Ali was unable to exist in a world where Ramazan screwed around in order to bring him plates of meze and a bit of spending money.

As for Ramazan, he could not bear Ali inhaling thinners, so he went out more and more often, and for longer hours, looking for custom. Seeing Ramazan go off to screw men and return with bruises on his neck and bite marks on his back made Ali resort even more to thinners, beer, wine, downers, and uppers.

As they hurtled in a downward spiral, Ramazan realized they would never recapture those first five days after Ali's return from the army. They could never have anything as good as that again. Why should they? What right did they have in their godforsaken world?

Ramazan understood everything, but what good was that? He did not want to leave Ali. No matter how much solvent Ali was inhaling, for Ramazan it was a panacea to know that some-body was waiting for him in the tiny room in Mirialem Street and that the somebody was Ali.

Without that, Ramazan could not cope or survive. Ali was inhaling so much solvent that there was no longer a single moment in the day when he was sober. Their room became a dump, and unless Ramazan brought food and forced it down him, Ali hardly ate at all. Even when he was asleep, there was always a bottle of thinner there, like a baby's feeding bottle. Ali would sleep fitfully with the bottle in his hand, the top stuffed with newspaper. Ramazan finally decided that the loneliness of being with Ali was unbearable and that he needed someone else around to bring Ali to his senses.

As Ramazan was wandering around Sultanahmet Park one day, he came across Recep, one of the boys who used to hang out at Surlar. Recep's situation had clearly deteriorated considerably. He had homeless written all over him. Everything about him, his clothes, head, eyes, hands, gave out the same message; and he smelled like a sewer.

"Hey, Recep! Come on, I'm taking you home with me. I'll give you a roof over your head, and tomorrow we'll find you a mattress in Topkapı. You can live with us on one condition."

"Whatever you say, Boss," said Recep. This semblance of respect was only because he had absolutely no hope of ever get-ting himself a job.

"You have to take care of Ali, as if he were a baby," said Ramazan. "He's really lost it. He's never without a bottle of thin-ner, and he's on pills the whole time. I'm taking you on as a nursemaid for Ali. That's the offer."

"It's a deal—apricots in Damascus!" they shouted simulta-neously, striking the air with their right hands.

It was a pledge. Recep had grown up with Ramazan's proverbs and sayings. Recep knew the Boss through and through, his sayings and everything about him. And so, Ali and Ramazan hit rock bottom, and Recep joined them as a sort of servant. At first, Ali did not like it at all. But Ramazan was out so much of the time and Ali was so lonely in that room that he started to enjoy having Recep there to keep an eye on him and create some sort of order around the place.

Ali grew to accept that Ramazan loved him so much that he had hired Recep to take care of him and see to his needs. And Ali needed taking care of. He realized that, and it made him feel guilty and ashamed. Oh, Ali! Is that the way to behave when you love someone?

VIOLENCE

15

"Something's going on around Taksim. It's corrupting the kids," Ramazan had said to Recep two days before. All the scum had turned up in Taksim. What were they doing, wandering around the park there?

He was feeling tense and depressed anyway. It wasn't working with Ali, but he could not live without him. Ali was like a thorn in Ramazan's side that caused pain with every movement and every breath. The pain was burning his soul.

"Ali, if only I could get you out of my system, then I could stop bleeding," thought Ramazan. "But I can't bear it without you. I'm obsessed with you, and you're obsessed with me." With these thoughts going around in his head, Ramazan found himself in Taksim, and he decided to go to nearby Gezi Park.

Ali had pulled himself together a bit since Recep came. He got some order into his life and cut down on the thinners, pills, and all that junk. He was keeping the room clean and taking care of himself.

Then, just when Ramazan thought Ali had stopped and was ready to find work, when it seemed he might start living like a human being—smash! He came crashing down again! Was Ramazan expected to look after him forever? This huge, strapping young man who, apart from working in the orphanage sweatshop, had never done a day's work in his life? Ali clung to Ramazan; he was completely dependent on him. Yet he inhaled thinners because of what Ramazan put him through: it was the only way! But Ramazan had to find the money for the pills, the thinners, and the drink. If Ramazan did not bring back money for food, clothes, coal, and the rent, what then? Ramazan had to keep taking care of Ali, which he found hard and depressing. Just that morning, they had had a fight, scuffling and shoving each other around. Thank God, Recep was there. Recep had intervened and, with some difficulty, managed to pull them apart. Sometimes, Ramazan was afraid that there would be blood: either Ali would kill him, or he would provoke Ali into such a fury that there would be an accident. "May God protect me from such a fate," thought Ramazan. Their situation was strange in that they seemed to love each other more intensely than ever. They were passionately in love and ever more addicted to that love. Every so often, Ali went through a crisis of remorse. He apologized over and over again for his addiction to thinners and drugs. "It's my fault, not yours, Ramazan," he said and, weeping with grief, collapsed onto their bed in sorrow. Ali started harming himself with a razor at times when he was very depressed and unable to speak to anyone. Ramazan could not believe that a person could abuse and despise himself so much. "What's wrong with you, Ali? You're the best, purest man in the world. You're worth a thousand of all those losers and maniacs out there." After Ali apologized and begged forgiveness, they made love, and

Ramazan felt as if his brain were rising up and hitting against the ceiling—boom, boom. Before this, they had devoured each other with their eyes in such a way that Recep thought it better to disappear. Recep did not reappear until noon the following day. He knew that when Ramazan and Ali made love, the world stopped for them and their passion transported them into another time zone. Ramazan was ensnared in a dreadful and increasingly tangled web with Ali.

"Goddamn you, Ali," said Ramazan. "I can't live with you, and I can't live without you! You beautiful jungle-bear, why the hell did you have to turn up at the orphanage!" Unaware of the effect all this pain was having on him, he walked toward Taksim. Ramazan needed to find work there. The clients were weird, the passersby were odd, and there were lots of women around. The place was teeming with women, as if all the city's chicks had poured in there to flaunt themselves. They kept looking at Ramazan, fixing their gaze on him as if they wanted to eat him raw. "Hey, what about picking up a chick? After all, if they're going to pay, why not?" he chuckled to himself.

As he laughed, an elderly queer came up to him. "Hello there, you magnificent boy. Aren't you a sight for sore eyes?" he said, winking at Ramazan. Ramazan shuddered with annoyance. The client was an irritating type with a goatee beard and silver-rimmed spectacles, smartly dressed in a leather jacket and casual trousers. That type had no idea of the cost of a fuck or anything else. They usually tried to take you back to their house and then demanded the full works. They would cling to Ramazan, begging him to stay. "Once more, once more," they would cry. "Like this. Now like that." No matter what he did, they would not leave him alone until he felt utterly wretched and debased. Ramazan had learned to recognize this type. They were the worst sort.

He much preferred to screw oafs like butchers, greengrocers, and family men.

"No way, I'd rather die," flashed Ramazan in reply with his catlike chuckle. Those types could not resist him when he laughed.

"Well, I'm ready if you are, so why not?" cackled the queer, with a smile like a wound across the middle of his face.

Ramazan felt his hackles rise. At least with oafs, you did not have to entertain them. Wham-bam and it was over with the fumblers. No need for appetizers or desserts. "Why should I?" he hissed.

The old queen was really groveling. "Because I'm handsome! Everything's in good condition." He reached out and gave a quick squeeze to Ramazan's bum. "Are you up for it?"

"Up for what? Fuck off!" said Ramazan, brandishing a switchblade, which he pulled out of his jacket pocket. Everything happened so fast that Ramazan could not believe it when he saw blood pouring out of the bastard. He knew nothing about knives or stabbing people; it was the first time he had taken the switchblade out with him. But this old queer had provoked him so much he just kept plunging the knife into him. The guy was staring in disbelief at the blood spurting out of his hand. "Gimme your wallet and your watch!" Ramazan was still angry with him. He had not killed the man, but he certainly wanted to get what he could out of him. Up for it, indeed? Who did the cunt think he was, squeezing his butt like that? "Goddamn it, you perv, you son of a bitch!" Ramazan filled his jacket pockets with whatever was in the guy's pockets, sizing up the situation as he did so. The man made no sound; he had soiled his clothes out of fear. Seeing urine seep on to the ground brought

Ramazan to his senses. He flung himself behind some bushes and started running for all he was worth toward the main street.

"Get him! Help! I'm dying! He-elp!" cried the man.

Ramazan crossed the main street and jumped into a taxi. "Mirialem Street, please."

"Which alem, son? Where's that?" said the elderly taxi driver turning around in surprise.

"Fındıkzade will do," gasped Ramazan. He was wiping his hands on his trousers and panting like a dog running for his life. Thankfully, the driver was half senile; a younger man might have understood what was going on. As they got nearer to home, Ramazan collected his thoughts and, cunningly, got out of the taxi in the main street so that the driver would not know where he lived. Just in case.

"Great, now the police are after you! You're a criminal! You've stabbed a man. So what happens next?" muttered Ramazan to himself as he walked the rest of the way home, still panting. Thankfully there was only Recep in the room, and he was sprawled out asleep and snoring like a pig, poor wretch! First Ramazan looked at the guy's watch; then he emptied his pockets out onto the table and turned the wallet inside out. There was a fair amount of money in it, enough to keep them for two or three weeks.

"So it was worth stabbing him," thought Ramazan, still feeling an uncontrollable anger toward the guy. He could not understand why his anger had not abated, even though he had spilled the man's blood. "Was I up for it, indeed! What a bastard! What an asshole!"

Recep woke up, horrified to see Ramazan talking to himself. "What is it, Boss? Have you done something bad?"

"How the hell would you know? You were fast asleep, weren't you?"

"I just know, Boss. I grew up with you, remember?"

Ramazan was exhausted, but he needed to pull himself together before Ali came back. He removed his jacket and trousers, rolled them into a ball, and sent Recep to put them out with the garbage.

"Boss, please don't do anything stupid. People are watching you. Honestly, everyone has their eye on you."

"Sooo?" said Ramazan.

"The evil eye is really after you, Boss. I'm scared something bad will happen to you one day because of the evil eye, something completely out of the blue. All because of the evil eye."

"Don't worry, kid," said Ramazan. "Worry doesn't stop things happening." He had no idea why he had said that. He crawled into Recep's bed in his underpants, hugged him tightly, and cried his heart out like a baby for ten or fifteen minutes. Why had he done that? Ramazan did not know. He had no answers to anything. But clouds of misfortune were hovering above his head. Something strange and evil was in the air. That much he knew for certain now. Ramazan cried a lot that day, mainly for himself. He cried and cried as if he could see what lay in store for him.

RETRIBUTION 16

For days, Ramazan did not set foot outside the door. The gravity of what he had done was gradually sinking in. He had stabbed a man! He had stuck a knife into a man! He could not remember how many times, but he hoped the old queer was not dead.

It had happened so close to the main street that somebody must have heard the cries for help. The guy must have been taken to hospital; they must have saved him. Surely it was not so easy to kill a man! Ramazan was surprised at how easily a man could be stabbed to death in broad daylight so close to Taksim Square. At the same time, he could not believe that he had gotten away with what he had done.

What the hell was going on? Days had passed and no police had come knocking at the door. Yet where would they find clues? Was the guy going to make a complaint anyway? What would he say to the police? "I tried to pick up a boy and made a pass at him." Is that what he would say? Would he even bother?

When Ramazan remembered what the man had said to him and how he had squeezed his backside, he flushed deeply and his hands made involuntary stabbing actions. Just as when he used to play marbles as a child and practice his imaginary strikes, now as he thought of those words and what had happened, his hands were practicing stabbing actions as if he had been stabbing people for years.

For the first week, he was paralyzed with fear. He holed himself up like a mouse. But by the second week, he gradually started to relax. However, he still tried not to go out. Just in case! They found a senile taxi driver to drive them around Fındıkzade for the essentials. It occurred to Ramazan that the great Turkish police probably did not have much time. After all, if they had to round up waifs and strays to beat and burn with cigarettes, would they bother to chase after some kid who had stabbed an old queer?

When Ramazan thought about how the policeman had beaten him to a pulp before stubbing out the cigarette on his neck, his hands started going again. He sat there, his hands and arms stabbing at imaginary bodies. While hiding in his hole after the attack, Ramazan realized for the first time how much anger he had stored up. How much violence was in him! How strong his desire was for revenge against Master and all the other assholes.

His state of mind was affecting his roommates as well. Their room was going from bad to worse. They piled newspapers under the chair with the broken leg. The sheets had not been washed for weeks, and the pillowcases and blankets smelled disgusting. As for the dishes, they were left in the sink for days at a time.

Ramazan yelled at Ali and Recep, "What sort of home is this? What kind of life is this? Fuck the pair of you! You're no use to anyone, you parasites." But mainly he went for Ali. Was this Ramazan's Arab, his obsessively clean childhood love who always had to be doing something? Who had single-handedly set about cleaning up the filth and stench left by Miss Nezahat? Who had brought peace and order to that wreck of an orphanage and turned it into a palace? Was this huffer, who could not even stand upright, the same boy?

Ramazan frequently smashed bottles of paint thinner and threw out any pills he found stashed away. And if Ali was completely out of it and sprawled on the sofa, he would set upon him, too. He hit out blindly with all his strength; he even kicked Ali.

Ali was obviously the stronger of the two and at least two heads taller than Ramazan, yet he cried, sobbed, apologized, and promised anything to make it stop. However, later, when he sobered up, Ali started to hit back at Ramazan, and Recep had difficulty prizing them apart. When they were going at each other like that, Recep caught the brunt of it and got covered in cuts and bruises.

Ramazan and Recep went out to buy a small carpet from a junk shop. They put sheets up at the windows, which had previously been covered with newspapers. Ramazan bought new sheets and pillows from Fatih Market, got Recep to wash the blankets and sweep the floor, and gave orders that the sink should be kept free of dirty dishes.

With some difficulty, Ramazan managed to get Recep and Ali to the hamam, where he hired an attendant to scrub them down and peel away almost two layers of skin. However, after their visit to the hamam, after the apartment was made spotless, and after being made to feel totally inadequate and useless, Ali shut down completely. He withdrew into his shell, refusing to speak, eat, smile, or sleep.

Ali paced about or wandered the streets aimlessly for hours at time. "Sad Owl has returned to the nest!" exclaimed Ramazan.

"Is His Excellency going to speak or smile this evening, I wonder? Do a cartwheel, Recep! Caoutchouc is like a flat tire. Do you think we can revive him by pumping him up?"

Ali looked at Ramazan angrily. He had never liked smutty jokes and found his homosexual tendencies hard to deal with; he was continually trying to suppress them. That night, Ali got mad and stormed out banging the door, leaving Ramazan to stew in his dirty jokes. Ramazan let him go. Ali always overreacted when he got mad. However, he hurled a stream of insults after Ali, because he could not bear it when Ali became distant and withdrew in that aloof way. But it was the middle of the night. What would happen to him? It was not like Ali to storm out like that without even taking a jacket. However, that night, he shot out of the house as if discharged by a fully wound spring. Ramazan stared after him. Ever since they had first set eyes on each other when Ali was brought to Mevlanakapı orphanage from Samandağı in Hatay province so that his relatives would not murder him, and ever since they had become an item as Ali and Ramazan, this was the first time that Ramazan had found himself left at home, on the bed, trying to sleep without Ali by his side. No sleepy eyes were waiting for him, no ears straining to hear his footsteps, no brokenhearted boy struggling with nightmares. It was the first time that Ali was out at night while Ramazan was at home. It was the first time that Ramazan was tossing and turning in bed waiting for Ali, wondering where he was. Where would Ali go? Ali, who had no one. Ali, who belonged only to Ramazan. Ali, who only existed when they were Ramazan and Ali.

"Where are you? What if the bears get you? What if they want to kidnap you because you're so beautiful?" Ramazan choked. He clenched his fists in pain. Ali's pain had come to choke him. "Why the hell didn't you keep your mouth shut? He's a sensitive kid, poor thing. I swear to God…" Ramazan muttered to himself.

"What's that, Boss?"

"I hurt Ali. Where can he be? You know he never goes out at night."

"I think he's coming. Listen, I can hear his footsteps." Ali staggered inside, blind drunk and stinking of alcohol and cigarettes. As he entered, he stumbled into the table by the door and fell groaning to the floor.

"Are you hurt, Ali?" asked Ramazan running to his side. He had never shown so much concern before. "Hey, what's this? You're covered in love bites! You son of a bitch, what have you been up to? Did you get laid? That's all we needed! Oh no, not that please!"

Ramazan started beating his head against the wall until it bled. Ali was curled up on the floor, vomiting and crying at the same time. Recep did not know whether to restrain Ramazan and stop him beating his head or to clean Ali up and comfort him. He ran from one side of their little cage of a room to the other.

"I didn't get laid, Ramazan. Honestly, I didn't do it. Believe me, I didn't. I just fucked him. So what! Isn't that what you do every Goddamn day? You do it with all sorts of people, every Goddamn day."

"Don't bring God into it!" spat Ramazan, suddenly sounding pious. "How could you do it? How? I was already a prostitute when I found you. I've always been a prostitute, that's my job. But you, you…" Ramazan collapsed in tears on the floor. Now they were both crying at opposite ends of the room. They were Ali and Ramazan again. They were complete once more. They had become one and returned to their true selves. They could not help it—there was no other way. They could not live as just Ali or just Ramazan. They could only exist as Ali and Ramazan, like Siamese lovers, cursed and blessed with love. But underneath, they were completely disintegrating.

BÜYÜKADA 17

Getting themselves back to rights was not easy and would take time; it was bound to take time. Who knew how long it would take? Ramazan could not stand the situation they were in, not knowing how long it would last, and always having to be the provider. He was not a patient person, and having to wait for some undefined period of time for things to improve was unbearable for him. Ramazan was unable to wait for anything. He could not bear the tyranny of time. There had been a chasm between them ever since the night when Ali had destroyed the magical spell of their relationship, their love for which there was no name.

Things improved slightly, of course. They no longer needled and provoked each other quite as much. Ali became silent and morose. He hardly touched solvents and had given up pills, wine, and beer—or so it seemed to Ramazan. Ali was looking for work. He threw himself into finding a job. After all, he was the man of the house. Ali now kept their home, or rather their little room, spotlessly clean and tidy, and he had taken to cooking strange dishes and concocting unusual meals.

He had no money, of course. Only what he could wangle out of Recep or earn himself. He even worked as a porter, carrying enormous loads on his back in Eminönü, Tahtakale, and Fatih Bazaar. But there was no other work—nothing at all. No work for a strapping young man with a primary school certificate and no work experience. All doors were closed to him. However hard Ali tried, however much he pleaded, he could not get a toehold in the job market. He was left out in the crushing vacuum of unemployment.

Ali was not the sort to canvass openly for work; he preferred to be more discreet about it. He could not work like Recep, as a sidekick to the messengers, agents, or middlemen in the Covered Bazaar. Even if he had wanted to, the moment they saw him they would have said, "No, man, we don't need anyone." There was not a hint of dishonesty or deceit about Ali. His face glowed with sincerity, decency, and goodness, but these were not sought-after qualities in the marketplace.

Ramazan could no longer endure the cleanliness and icy atmosphere at home; the silences and all the subtle manifestations of blame had become too oppressive. He called up his army friend Timucin who, when they went their different ways, had said, "Call me if ever you want work as a waiter." Timo had spent two seasons as an *İstanbullu* waiter. His grandfather had been a waiter in Samatya, where his father was still a headwaiter. Timo liked to spend the summers working as a waiter on Büyükada, the largest of the Princes' Islands. He spent his winters at the café where his father worked, so working on Büyükada was like a summer holiday and a tonic to him. "Sure, Ramo," said Timucin. "I'm starting at the Kapris, right by the quay on Büyükada. I'll sound out the owner; if he needs anyone, you should come and show your face here on the island." It was nearly the end of spring, which suited Ramazan because it was the best time for hiring waiters. It turned out that they really did need another waiter. The owner accepted Ramazan immediately when he heard he had trained as a waiter in the Turkish Army. When Ramazan entered the Kapris restaurant, he smiled broadly at Timo and said, "Good to see you!"

Ramazan was put to work immediately. He liked being called Ramo; he suddenly had a new identity on Büyükada. The Islands were teeming with rich kids and kids from good families—Jewish kids, politicians' kids, businessmen's kids, and college kids. On most days, these youngsters would congregate in the early evening in the square by the quay. However, the Kapris Restaurant was not really their style; it was a bit shabby and dated, rather too Turkish. They preferred the patisseries that stood on three sides of the square, with their famous profiteroles, and the café in the far corner that welcomed everyone alighting from the ferry with the offer of a beer. The youngsters rolled around from one place to another, putting on airs and graces, looking like exotic marbles. Ramazan played a new game of marbles with these young boys. When he escaped from his duties as a waiter, he spent his time swimming and sunbathing, strolling about and exchanging glances. In fact, he was starting to pick up a lot of work. Ramazan was hardly sleeping. He was on the go the whole time, working round the clock. It was difficult to get these gentlemen's sons used to the idea of paying. They thought Ramo was after them for their clean underpants, their aftershave, their tight-fitting clothes, or their parents' positions. Oh no! But Ramazan persevered with them. He explained sweetly that they had to pay; they were getting a professional service. They would find no one else to do it for them, for all their styled hair, almond eyes, and the influential families that they did not deserve. He played with them, made fun of them, and heaped insults on them. Once a few of these dandies finally realized that there was nothing exceptional about them and that there were people who actually made a living in this way, the rest was easy. Ramazan's reputation spread, not only on Büyükada but all the Islands. The rich kids got huge excitement from playing around and coupling with each other, despite the fact that outwardly they appeared squeaky clean. Ramo had turned up in their lives like a whirlwind of sexual desire, and they flocked to him in droves.

"If I don't keep going, I'll lose face! I'm scared that one day I'll drop dead in their hands or on top of them. I've become nothing more than a petrol pump, Timo!"

"Some of them are weirdly girl-like. Bring a few of them to me. You can't take care of all of them," said Timo. "We just have to close our eyes and do our job."

"That's easy to say," retorted Ramazan. "But I've spent my life doing this. I've graduated from being a child prostitute to a Büyükada petrol pump attendant."

"Oh yeah," said Timo. "Well, you will keep sticking out your ass."

"That's OK," replied Ramazan. "These queers choose you for your ass. If you have a flabby backside, they don't find you attractive. With the right equipment in front and a good butt, you're in."

Ramo, the new Ramazan, started wearing stylish designer T-shirts, short-sleeved shirts, and blue jeans given to him by the rich kids.

"Who would have thought this place was full of queers! And they're all from well-off families!" exclaimed Timo, who was now beyond joking and venturing into the envy zone.

"Yeah, and especially the Jews and Armenians, who are made to get engaged in high school to ensure they marry their own kind," said Ramazan. "They're not going to say to their parents, 'Mommy, Daddy, I'm gay. There's no point in all this; we should stop the family line here.' The Turkish kids are just the same. They have rich girls hanging around their necks, but these queers are up to their necks in lies and deceit. They're worn out from fucking each other, and they know exactly what they're doing."

"Thanks to Ramo!" shouted Timo. It was not long before Timo started getting work with Ramazan's leftovers. The environment was good, the money was great; furthermore, he was gradually starting to enjoy screwing boys. "Hey, what if I'm gay?" Timo asked himself. He was too embarrassed to ask Ramo. Ramo might have retorted, "Of course you are!" or "Wake up— what's the big deal? Have you only just realized?" Then there would be no going back; nobody would believe Timo was not gay, including himself. Especially himself.

Ramazan went home for a visit every two or three weeks. He dragged himself there reluctantly, because Ali was falling apart. Ramazan knew he would swear at Ali and drive him to distraction, yet he did not want to hurt his Bear-cub anymore. He did not want to cause Ali to sink any lower into his inner depths, down into the pit of his soul. Ramazan knew very well how dark and deep the pit in Ali's soul was. If Ali ventured down there, nobody would ever be able to get him out again. Ramazan knew that Ali would not survive those depths. He could not be allowed to go there. Ali tried to behave well; he was always good-natured and patient. He seemed to have no idea that Ramazan had now become Ramo. The worst thing was seeing how pleased Ali was with the Büyükada version of Ramazan, as if unaware that

Ramazan was counting the seconds until he could escape from their little room. Ali was resigned to his fate, in his own perceptive and naturally decent way.

"Ali, you are as patient as I am impatient," thought Ramazan on the ferry back to the island. "You are as clean as I am dirty. I'm tainted, while you're true as a block of wood, a cave, a mountain, or a forest." Ramazan burned inside, wishing he had spoken these fine words to Ali. Later, this was to wrench his heart when he thought of Ali in the final moments of his life. Ali had no need to utter fine words. Ali never got angry, never treated Ramazan badly. Except for once, when he had pushed Ramazan away out of frustration, as if to say, "Is this what you want from me?" But he had done it in a state of shame and sorrow. Ali had never done any wrong to Ramazan. Maybe it was wrong for Ali and Ramazan to be together. Ali believed in fate, and Ramazan was his fate. He believed Ramazan was the best that could happen to him, simple as that. "Aliiiii!" Ramazan wanted to cry with love and remorse on the return ferry. But the moment he set foot on the quayside, he became Ramo and was transformed into a predatory monster. That was Ramazan; he was like that.

"That's how God made him," Ali would say tenderly. "What can Ramazan do? He can't help it."

WOMAN 18

By the time summer was drawing to an end, Ramo and Timo, the two penniless sharp-dressing waiters from the Kapris Restaurant, were on intimate terms with the rich kids. One of them generously invited them to his sister's birthday party. The party was on a Friday evening, the worst night of the week for waiters the world over. In their profession, it is the night when they are required to work most.

As if that were not enough, middle-aged men and women came flooding into the restaurant that night as if they had been waiting for it all summer. They sat there eating and drinking to excess and talking at the tops of their voices. It was too much! Midnight had arrived by the time Ramazan was able to get away from work. "Let's not go, Timo," he yawned. "What'll happen if we turn up at this time of night? What do their birthdays mean to us?"

"Man, it's at this time of night that things get warmed up. These kids get into little groups and start messing around with each other, didn't you know that? Come on, don't back out now.

Let's go and see what's going on. They asked us to a party, Ramo! We're in with them; they'll never get rid of us now. We'll be here, year after year after year…"

"We'll end up getting our pension from fucking on Büyükada at this rate! God forbid! These rich bastards have been getting me down for a while now. They've sucked me dry."

"Please, as a favor to me! Come on, quick march! Aren't we friends anymore? Get up, we're going."

Timo persisted so much that Ramazan gave in for the sake of friendship. He did not feel inclined to go, despite the company they would be mixing in. But he knew very well what Timo's problem was. It was obvious. One of the rich queers had a real thing for Timo and vice versa. He would sit in the café opposite the Kapris for hours every day exchanging glances and smiles with Timo. They were always finding some pretext or other to go over and see each other.

Timo had no wish to face up to his homosexuality or to fall in love with some rich bastard! "It means nothing, Ramo," he would say. Yet the only reason Timo was pestering Ramazan to go out to a party at that time of night, when they were both worn out, was to satisfy his own cravings. But falling in love is fraught with danger—Ramazan knew that better than anyone.

It took half an hour to get to the house. When they found it, all they could say was, "Wow!" Was it a villa, a mansion, a palace? Bloody hell! A man opened the outer gate and took them along a winding path to the boathouse next to the villa's private jetty. Dawn was about to break, and the two good-for-nothings had no idea what they were doing there. But that is what they had been told—the birthday party was being held in the boathouse, and the parents were sleeping up in the villa.

Ramazan immediately collapsed on the edge of a sofa in the corner with the intention of stretching out quietly and going to sleep. Timo would wake him when he wanted to leave. The rich bastards were already befuddled and lolling around all over the place. Timo immediately made a beeline for his boyfriend. Through half-closed eyes, Ramazan saw them leaving the room together hand in hand. But he was so sleepy that his reactions were slow. He said nothing. And if he had? What difference would it have made? He was hardly going to ask Timo to come back and sing him a lullaby. Ramazan leaned back and settled himself comfortably on the sofa. He was suddenly overwhelmed by drowsiness and sleep was taking over.

"Hey look, there's my brother's friend Ramo. It is you, isn't it? Ramo—the one my brother never stops talking about?" A girl sat down at the other end of the sofa and put her hand on his knee. She talked as if Ramazan were a puppet that just needed its strings pulling to wake him up and bring him to life.

Ramazan opened his eyes wide and looked at the girl. How pale her face was! How had she managed to resist being out in the sunshine all summer? Her hair was a strange yellowish color and hung down below her shoulders. It was probably dyed; he had no idea whether women had hair this color in real life.

What did Ramazan know about women? He had always seen them, looked at them, from a distance. The only one he knew was their primary school teacher. He knew Miss Nevin. They were such strange creatures. He understood and liked them in the way he understood and liked cats. Ali loved cats and dogs. If Ramazan had let him, he would have brought several of them home.

"Aren't we chatty tonight?" The girl put her arm through his. She was very drunk; her eyes were unfocused, and her words were slurred. All that remained of the lipstick she had been wearing was a red rim around the lips. How ugly her lips and mouth were! Ramazan pulled a face without realizing it.

"What? Do I disgust you? I am disgusting, aren't I? Dis*gust*ing!" The girl began crying into Ramazan's lap. Ramazan could not believe the speed at which things seemed to be happening. The girl had even started to grope him through his trousers. Ramazan hardened despite the revulsion he felt. He was afraid he would be unable to escape her hands. He did not know how he was supposed to talk to her or what he was supposed to do. He was afraid of appearing uncouth or clumsy, so he sat there motionless as the girl lifted her head and plunged her tongue into his mouth.

She pulled Ramazan into a bedroom, locked the door behind them, threw herself on the bed, and started to remove her clothing. Ramazan was disgusted by the smell of alcohol on her breath and the smell of drink, cigarettes, and hashish that oozed from every part of her body; he feared he would throw up.

Ramazan was so afraid that his fatigue, confusion, and revulsion would make him vomit that he jumped on top of the girl and began screwing her. Afraid that the girl would cry or make a scene, he did it automatically, hardly knowing what he was doing. Automatically, he turned her over so as not to see her face.

The girl yelled so loudly with pleasure that Ramazan felt embarrassed and ejaculated early. The first time in his professional life! "Come on, come on! Again! Take me!" cried the girl, writhing on the bed. Ramazan looked in horror at her face and her body, as if he were seeing some sort of animal species for the first time in his life. She was flailing about and screeching as if she had just emerged from the depths of an ocean or a swamp.

She took Ramazan between her lips. Ramazan wished he could cut off his penis to escape the girl's mouth. He wished he could throw himself off the jetty into the sea for having had an erection.

To punish himself for this, he shut his eyes and, with some trepidation, took the girl from the front. This time, there was no question of premature ejaculation. Ramazan kept himself going like a well-oiled mechanical pump as the girl yelled and moaned. Finally, unable to bear the torture any longer, he faked an ejaculation and withdrew. He jumped up and put his trousers on; he was still wearing his T-shirt anyway.

"Ah, may I ask you for the fee?" he said, as the girl was getting herself together. It was the first time he had used the words *fee* or *may* in a professional situation.

"Whaat?" squealed the girl. "What fee? What are you talking about, Ramo? You are joking, aren't you? Come on, let's go for a swim. We can make love in the sea. Come on."

Ramazan bit his lips to stop himself saying, "Didn't your brother tell you, you spoiled brat? He's paid my visiting fee at least twenty times since the start of summer." Ramazan was unable to act normally with types like this. He had no idea what the hell to expect. "God help me!" he said, as he unlocked the door.

"Is that all? What do you mean? You fuck me and throw me away? Didn't you like me? Wasn't I any good?" she said, starting to cry. Ramazan stared at her in horror for a few more moments and then made a run for it. It took him exactly four and a half minutes to reach the outer gate at the top of the hill.

He was out of breath when he reached the gate, but he kept running. Looking back every so often to see if any naked creatures were chasing him with long-fingered hands ready to dig into his back, he ran for his life until he reached his room at the back of the restaurant.

Having to screw that swamp girl at the birthday party had disgusted Ramazan so much that it had tainted everything about Büyükada. From then on, all his rich young clients seemed to have her smell and taste about them. After all, this was Ramazan's profession, and he had to maintain a degree of self-respect and certain standards! He had no wish to do this job if it was so difficult and disgusting. Ramazan sighed with relief when the Kapris closed at the end of September. He had certainly made good money, but they had screwed up his soul. He felt as if he had been torn apart and turned into something alien. These people had filled Ramazan with even more resentment and hatred. Why were they so rich and people like him so poor? The impossibility of answering this question was driving him mad, and it became increasingly difficult to keep up any pretense that he enjoyed being with those rich bastards.

Ramazan returned to Mirialem Street an even angrier young man than before. Ali reacted to Ramazan's anger with a silent, animal-like sorrow, certain in the knowledge that things could not carry on like that. Anything bad that happened to Ramazan was also bad for Ali. They understood each other so intimately that Ali knew Ramazan would pay a price for his mounting anger. It was just a matter of time. What an anger it was! Like a volcano waiting to erupt. But life never stops; it comes at us from all directions. Ali was having terrible nightmares. Every night, he dreamed their house was being flooded and they were being washed away. He woke up suffocating and struggling for air, thinking he was drowning. Sometimes, Ramazan woke him.

"What is it? Are you having another nightmare, Jungle-bear? Mister Caoutchouc, what's the matter with you? Don't they ever stop? Can't you ever be at ease?"

"I can," said Ali looking lovingly at Ramazan. "I'm at ease with you. Anything else in this world is a lie. This is the best there is. There's nothing else I want."

FAVOR

Winter was approaching, and it was getting very cold. Sensing their inevitable doom, Ali knew there was only one way to avoid feeling the cold and to contain his distress at Ramazan working day and night as a male prostitute—oh, there were so many reasons for Ali to resort to thinners and pills. He did not count up the reasons; he just kept inhaling thinners and popping pills in order to blot them out. He was not obliged to provide a list of reasons to anyone. Ali understood Ramazan so well. Just as he had showed understanding toward Ramazan ever since the day they had left Master's sofa bed in the early hours of the morning as kids, so Ramazan had to accept that Ali needed thinners to live. There was no other option.

One Sunday, there was a southerly wind that gave a false sense of spring. Everyone welcomed this pleasant break right at the start of winter, and the whole population of Istanbul seemed to be out in the streets enjoying themselves. Ramazan dashed out early that morning, partly because he had become extremely energetic and active, and partly because he could not bear to see

Ali getting high on thinners. Ramazan wandered aimlessly for a while. He screwed one guy at a dreadful hotel in Sirkeci. He then turned down an unsavory-looking character on Gülhane Rise—the son of a bitch tried to drive too hard a bargain! "Are you blind or something? No one with any taste would offer that sort of money. Idiot! Cunt!" said Ramazan as he headed for Sultanahmet Square, still fuming at the man.

Ramazan went to sit in one of the tea gardens overlooking the square. He was sipping his tea and playing with a toasted sandwich that was going cold when he saw Miss Nurşin in the distance. At first he did not recognize her. He screwed up his eyes but could not quite make her out. He looked hard again, searching his memory. Yes, it was Miss Nurşin! But how she had changed! Could this be the beautiful young woman he had last seen three or four years ago at the orphanage? Is this what she had become? She looked as though she had been ravaged by life for months, or years. As if she had suffered terrible betrayal and neglect. Miss Nurşin now seemed shrouded in fatigue and despair. Only her honey-colored eyes were the same. They still had a look of childlike innocence.

"Ah, is that you, Ramazan? Come and sit here. Aren't you handsome? Of course, you were always a beautiful child, and now you've become a splendid young man. Come, let me give you a kiss." Ramazan was cornered. It had taken him so long to recognize Miss Nurşin and take in all the changes that he was unable to make his getaway in time.

He found himself politely sipping tea with Miss Nurşin. "Ali's not too bad, miss. Could be better—but there's no work. Unemployment is a bit of a problem."

"Ah, dear Ali! In all my years in education, I never came across another child like Ali. He had such intelligence and sensitivity, such a wish for self-understanding—Ali was something special. Ramazan dear, please say hello from Miss Nurşin. Tell him I send my love. Give him a hug and kiss from me."

"Of course, miss. And you? Are you all right?" Ramazan said this merely as a courteous response to the nice words she had said about Ali; there was no hidden agenda. Later, he would be unable to forgive himself.

"Me, Ramazan? Me? Am I all right? Do I even exist? Who am I? Let me start at the beginning. But not over tea. Come, let's go somewhere else and have a beer. We're friends now, so call me Nurşin, no more 'miss,' for heaven's sake."

They crossed the road and went to a beer house that was mainly filled with penniless, drunken tourists. Miss Nurşin downed nine beers, one after the other! As she drank, she cried, talked, explained, and cried again. The one thing that remained of the Miss Nurşin from their orphanage days was her beautiful almond-shaped eyes. "Shall we go to a hotel, Ramazan?" she pleaded with those eyes, as Ramazan struggled manfully with his second beer. "Please, make love to me. That man ruined me. At the end of five years, five wasted years, he went off leaving a note on the table, like a bit of loose change!"

Ramazan had already been listening for two hours to Miss Nurşin relating the cruelty, treachery, and hypocrisy of the married man who had abandoned her, and how bad the last five years had been for her. She went on and on until Ramazan was afraid he was about to explode.

"In his note, he even put his apostrophes in the wrong place. And he wrote 'onto' when it should have been 'on to.' Can you believe it, Ramazan? Should I have forgiven him? You wouldn't do that, would you?"

Ramazan wondered if Miss Nurşin would have felt better if the man had known his grammar, or had gone without leaving a note at all. He could not believe that a good-looking young woman could turn up out of the blue and insist on going to bed with him just because some bastard had trampled over her and bulldozed through her life with his lies. The woman probably had a curse on her. He shuddered as he suddenly remembered the swamp girl on Büyükada.

"What's the matter? I'm embarrassing you. You find me hateful and disgusting, don't you? Tell me, please. I'm a psychologist," she said, her almond eyes filling with tears. She took hold of one of Ramazan's hands and raised it to her heart, her breast. Her tears were falling on his hand.

"Come on then, miss. There's quite a decent hotel just around the corner. We'll go there." Ramazan went to bed with Miss Nurşin because it was the only way to escape her hand, and he felt sorry for her. With her, he wanted to atone for his shame over the recent experience with the girl on Büyükada. Also, of course, he did it for Ali. Ramazan was able to do a favor for Miss Nurşin, whom Ali had loved, respected, and idolized for so many years. It was a gesture of self-sacrifice. All these feelings were mixed up inside Ramazan. Whatever the reasons, he had gone with Miss Nurşin to a hotel room in Sultanahmet where they did it three times. It was to make her feel better—and she did. By the end of their hour in the hotel, the shroud of drunkenness, unhappiness, humiliation, and worthlessness seemed to lift from Miss Nurşin. She seemed more like her old self—younger, prettier, better in every way. Miss Nurşin had a long, long shower and then slowly dressed, talking all the time. But her talk was now like the twittering of birds.

Finally, she took her purse out of a cloth bag with a picture of a cat on it and emptied out all the money. "Here, Ramazan dear. Don't think I didn't know you do this for a living. But you were so good for me, I think I'll give you the necklace that bastard gave me as well." She pointed to her neck where a fine gold chain with six golden cats was hanging.

Ramazan flushed bright red. "No, miss! I could never take it!" he cried, dashing out of the room.

Miss Nurşin ran after him, gathering her things together at the same time. "Ramazan. Stop, wait for me!"

She caught up with him in front of the hotel. "Please, give me your telephone number. We can do this again, can't we, darling?"

"But, miss…" At that very moment, Ramazan noticed Recep standing on the other side of the road, staring at them as if he had seen a forest fire. Recep must have seen them both come out of the hotel, seen Ramazan go bright red. He would have realized that some weird scene was being played out between them, and he had enjoyed it. The only way that Ramazan could think of to escape Miss Nurşin forever was to embrace that little sneak Recep, who was watching them with a big grin on his face. "Hey, Recep. What are you doing here at this time of day, man?"

Miss Nurşin called, "Hi, Recep. Are you OK?" before disappearing from sight.

Ramazan went shoved Recep away. "Forget anything you saw. Whatever you thought happened, wipe it, you Kurdish moron! I'll forget it, too. I was just doing a favor. It was a bit of self-sacrifice. We'll both forget about it."

Recep was laughing beneath his mustache, as if to say, "So what? We all have the right to a bit of self-sacrifice, don't we? You can't kid me." Indeed, unable to keep his mouth shut, Recep said as much later on.

"Shut up. So I did it, but it doesn't mean you have to do the same. It's complicated. This women business is different. They screw you up. God save us from the lot of them!" said Ramazan, brushing off his jacket collar with his hand as they walked home. Later he took off the jacket and gave it to Recep. "You said you liked it. Take it, it's yours. But for goodness sake, don't say anything. Not to anyone. Promise me…"

"Do you think I don't get it? I won't tell Ali. Of course I get it. I'm not an idiot, am I?" grinned Recep in his special nasty, sly way.

RECEP 20

Recep was a Kurd from Van in eastern Turkey. A *Vanlı* Kurd. His birth certificate gave his birthplace as Van, but who knows where a kid brought up in an orphanage came from? Nobody knew who his mother and father were or where they originated.

Shortly after Recep went to live with Ali and Ramazan in Fındıkzade, he succeeded in finding a niche for himself in the Covered Bazaar, serving glasses of tea to nearby shops. Because he was alert and amenable, and because he was Recep, he became a messenger for the stall holders. He was promoted to fetching and carrying for them because he entertained them and made them laugh. It was during that time that he discovered his Van identity, his Kurdish identity, which gave him a feeling of belonging. Recep became a "somebody," and it was good for him. The more he realized this, the more *Vanlı* and Kurdish he became, even though he did not know a single word of Kurdish.

Despite having grown up as a member of the tribe of urban orphans, Recep started to pretend it was otherwise, as if he had come by bus from Van to Topkapı station and been introduced to

Istanbul only a month or even a week before. Recep perfected the role of a funny, innocent boy from Van, who had only just joined the ranks of big city dwellers.

Not content with remaining a messenger, Recep wanted to advance in every way. Having adopted a Kurdish persona, he put it to work and rose to become a bargaining agent for the Van and Siirt monopolies. He was going onward and upward. The more Kurdish Recep became, the more he rose within his social class. As this happened, he started to ruffle Ali and Ramazan, especially Ramazan. Slowly, Recep became more assertive and impatient with the other two, but as in his work, it happened very gradually. Throughout his childhood, Recep had been Ramazan's sidekick and errand boy. When he encountered true gentlemen and got to know the Kurdish market bosses, he felt ashamed at having been a queer's toy, even if it was in the past, and at being trained by a prostitute whom he had unsuccessfully tried to imitate for so many years.

The more shame Recep felt, the more he hated Ramazan. While Ramazan was on Büyükada, Recep and Ali had established a fairly good relationship. Ali was a spotlessly clean individual who was in love, rather than a homosexual. Even Recep had to admit that Ali was a careful, thoughtful, and sensitive fellow. However, Recep grew tired of Ramazan and Ali's endless bickering, with their arguments, sorrows, and lovesickness. Also, even though he would not admit it, they made him jealous. Recep no longer suited their purpose; he was no longer prepared to be Ali's nurse or to be constantly at Ramazan's beck and call.

Within a few days of Recep seeing Ramazan and Miss Nurşin leaving that hotel together (ooh-aah!), the tables were turned completely. The weather was overcast that day, and Ramazan was finding it difficult to get up. He had a fever and sore throat and had obviously caught a chill. He did not want to go out at all, let alone look for work, but he knew he had to eat and, more importantly, drink something.

"Make me some soup, Ali," said Ramazan hoarsely, wondering why they could not show even a little respect to the head of the household. He felt offended by the lack of decent service offered to him. Ali stared at Ramazan blankly. Clearly, the only thing Ali wanted was to go out and find some thinner.

Ramazan turned to Recep, who had been wearing his favorite jacket nonstop since seeing him with Miss Nurşin. This new Kurd, this fake *Vanlı*, was not the old Recep they loved. Ramazan could no longer trust him or feel completely at ease with him. Recep had now become a Kurd, while Ali and Ramazan remained orphans. Recep belonged somewhere; he had a city, even if it was in ruins. However, Ali and Ramazan had nothing between them; they belonged nowhere and nowhere belonged to them. These feelings built up and intensified but were never articulated. There was no outward sign of Ramazan and Ali's disintegration, but inwardly they were being torn apart.

"What's the matter with the pair of you?" complained Ramazan. "Don't you care at all? Who brings in the rent, huh? Who buys the food and drink? Oh, so sorry Recep Boss, were you sleeping? Even the jacket you're wearing is a present from me, isn't it?"

"What present, Ramazan Boss? Where I come from, it's called hush money."

"Fuck you and your hush money! Can't you do anything right, you two-faced Kurdish cuckold! Turncoat Kurd! You try and make us believe you're a true Kurd—as if we'd buy that. You're nothing but chicken feed!"

These references to his Kurdishness made Recep very angry; it was like having his most sacred treasure spat upon. He could control his feelings for a short while, but not for long. It was clear that the two of them would soon come to blows.

"What do you mean by that? I'm a *Vanlı*, aren't I? God only knows what's on your birth certificate. I bet they put Pimpistan as your birthplace, or wherever it is that prostitutes hang out! Hell, you even screwed our psychologist Miss Nurşin for money! For fucking money! Poor Ali, he really loved our Miss Nurşin."

Hearing her name mentioned twice, Ali realized the seriousness of the quarrel, but it was only with these last words that he woke up to the full horror of it. "What's that? Ramazan and Miss Nurşin? Ramazan, say something. Is he telling the truth? Did you do that to me? Ramazan?"

"Stop saying, 'Ramazan, Ramazan' like that! Yeah! I did it! I felt sorry for her and I did it. I didn't take any money. I did it because I knew you liked her so much."

"Be-be-because I liked her? You went and fucked the teacher as a favor to me?" Ali's voice rose and then faded to a whisper. "I told her everything that happened to me. She was the only person I ever told." He grabbed a bread knife from the sink and thrust it into Ramazan's chest.

Ali had stabbed Ramazan. It was so sudden and unexpected that the three of them just stood there looking at the flow of blood. Ramazan pressed his hand over the place where he had been stabbed, but the blood continued to gush out. Ali fell to the ground with his head between his hands. "*Yemooo! Yemooo! Yemooo!*" He was cradling himself as he called out for his mother. "*Veynik yemooo? Veynik?* Where are you, Mother? Mother? Where have you gone?"

Recep picked up Ramazan and, holding him by the arms, took him outside. There he threw Ramazan into one of the taxis waiting at the corner. "Cerrahpaşa Hospital," said Recep to the driver. "Hurry. For God's sake, be quick. It's a matter of life and death." Within ten minutes, Ramazan was at the emergency entrance of Cerrahpaşa Hospital. The nurses whisked him off to an operation room where the doctors immediately anaesthetized him. Everything happened so quickly, it was like a film. Ramazan could not tell what was real and what was imaginary. Ali had stabbed him! It had come to that! Yes, even that happened to Ali and Ramazan. They never saw Kurdish Recep again. He did not even come back for his few clothes and bits of bedding. He had abandoned them to a loneliness that would last forever. Forever? Their time had come, and they were waiting.

WOUND

Ramazan had been lying with his eyes open for half an hour when two policemen came up to his bed. "Sir, who stabbed you? You are going to press charges, aren't you?" they asked politely. Ramazan could not help thinking they were teasing him. They had sent two such upright, polite, and handsome policemen! These two gentlemen were expressing sympathy and advising Ramazan to launch a complaint against the person who had stabbed him. "Trust us, sir. We have experience. Whoever did this will undoubtedly do it again. Give us a name and make a statement. Otherwise the matter will only escalate further, and neither you nor the perpetrator will get over it."

"No, sir," said Ramazan. "It's nothing. I was in a rage and stabbed myself. You can put that down in your file. Just leave it at that." Ramazan stubbornly refused to change his statement. Why would he give them Ali's name? Would he ever launch a complaint against Ali? Against the love of his life?

Ramazan could not believe what had happened. Ali had actually stabbed him, his Ali who was normally so docile, sensitive, and polite, and who was so desperately in love with Ramazan. Ali had bottled things up until he snapped. In the end he could take no more. He just could not tolerate Ramazan being a prostitute.

Yet if Ramazan did not work as a prostitute, how were they to manage? What would Ali do for thinners? And how would he get hold of his pills and alcohol? Where would he sleep? It was absolutely true that Ramazan had slept with Miss Nurşin because he felt sorry for her. He had done it as a favor. Whatever Ramazan said, Ali would never believe him, even if he swore in God's name that he had done it because Ali cared so much for Miss Nurşin. Not only as a favor to her, but also as a favor to Ali. Anyway, he was already a gigolo. That was his job! He had not yet gotten over the swamp girl on Büyükada. But what difference did one more make? This time it was on the house.

The reasons were all very complicated and confused; he went over them again and again during the eight days he lay in the hospital, without managing to resolve a single one. However, whenever Ramazan thought of Ali, these reasons seemed meaningless. Ramazan was fully aware of the anger that Ali had been harboring for so many years in his patient and forbearing way.

Ramazan felt crushed and small in his hospital bed at the thought that Ali was right. If he had been able, he would have run up to Ali, saying, "Forgive me, Ali!" He would have gone out into the streets searching for Ali, even if it had meant bursting his stitches. These were Ramazan's thoughts as he lay in the hospital, but he knew very well that Ali was not at home waiting for him. If he had been waiting for him, if everything had been all right, then Ali would have come rushing to the hospital. Maybe Ali would have asked for forgiveness, maybe not. But he would have come to the hospital.

One day passed, then two days passed, and still Ali did not appear. Ramazan knew then that, however often he looked toward the door as everyone else's visitors passed in and out of the ward, Ali would not come. Ramazan knew that he had gone. So, Ali had left! He had disappeared from Ramazan's life.

How would Ali take care of himself? What could he do? How would he earn a living? Ali was a mess; he was in pieces. Ramazan worried about him as if he were a baby. He knew that this was not the end, that neither of them had anyone else. They were still Ali and Ramazan, and it was inevitable that they would make up. He could sense this.

But there were moments when Ramazan had doubts. They were unbearable moments that tore at his insides, making him miserable with anxiety, yearning, and sorrow. It was as if a hundred crows were taking off from branches inside him and cawing at each other before alighting on other branches.

Ramazan kept seeing crows in his dreams. His dreams always involved crows. What did crows signify? Why were they pestering him?

Caw caw, said the crows / See that bough, take a look / So a good look I took / Oh foolish crows!

He kept recalling this stupid song from primary school days. Why did he have to keep remembering it? Then he would ignore the crows and allow them to disperse. But if he tried to erase them from his mind, they returned, cawing and flapping their wings.

Ramazan had many dreams like that in the hospital. The bulging radiators in the wards were kept at a very high temperature. Ramazan was not used to such heat, nor was his body used to such a comfortable bed and bedding. Ramazan slept to escape

Ali's sorrow, but the crows immediately started flying about in his dreams. For days and nights, he struggled with them.

"What is it with these crows?" thought Ramazan, with the grim realization that he could no longer end his question with Caoutchouc, Cave-boy, Jungle-bear, Fellah, or any of his other pet names for Ali. Ramazan now felt ashamed about all the names he had used for Ali. He used to call him by any name that came into his head! What a lot Ali had had to put up with! He had accepted so much without complaint. Clearly his breaking point had been Miss Nurşin. And Ramazan thought he had done a favor for Ali with his generosity to Miss Nurşin.

"She was the only person I ever told," Ali had said, just before the knife incident. Ali's childhood had been so full of pain and horror that he could not talk about it to anyone else.

Then Ramazan recalled their first night together, when he had not even bothered to ask, "What does *yemoo* mean, Ali?" He had guessed it meant "mother." But would it have hurt to ask Ali? He was always so insensitive and arrogant toward Ali.

Ramazan grew depressed in the overheated room that he was sharing with three others. The other patients always had visitors coming and going, bringing pastries, cakes, cologne, and flowers. Not a single person came to see Ramazan. Not even Ali. During that week, while Ramazan was confined to his hospital bed, he understood the true value of Ali. It was something he had refused to acknowledge until then. Ramazan understood the value of being "Ali and Ramazan." He was nothing without Ali. Not even half or quarter of a person. Ramazan was nothing, nothing at all.

In the early hours of the morning, he would suddenly wake up and start searching for Ali, forgetting that he was in the hospital and that Ali was not by his side. Ali had stabbed him, which was why he was lying in Cerrahpaşa Hospital. Ali was not at home waiting for Ramazan. Ali had packed and left. In the early hours of the morning, Ramazan would wake up and the reality would hit him. Then he felt like howling. "Aliiiii!" he moaned, wanting to howl like a wolf. But Ramazan was in the hospital, and there were other people sleeping in the same room. "Big boys don't cry." It was a nasty saying that people were always using. Ramazan had used it to taunt Ali whenever he cried. "What a bastard you are, Ramazan," he thought. "You come out with things without listening to what you're saying. You really made the kid suffer." Realizing he was referring to Ali as "the kid" made Ramazan feel terrible. He swore that he would become a completely reformed Ramazan as soon as he got out of hospital. He would find Ali, give up prostitution, and do whatever it took. Ramazan would be a real man, and he would make a man of Ali, too. No thinners or anything like that! Ramazan kept making promises like this to himself. It made him feel better when he made these pledges. Then he would start to doze and drift off into a sound sleep, that is, if the crows did not bother him. If the crows started pestering him, he would sleep badly. "What is it with these crows? Where are you, Ali? Come and shoo away these black pests. Take me in your arms. Make me go to sleep. Yes? Will you, Ali?" Would he?

R E U N I O N 22

Ali had swept, dusted, and cleaned every corner of their room before he packed his things and left, just as Ramazan had expected. After Ramazan returned to their little room, he found that he actually missed the hospital. The crows and waking up alone in a sweat without Ali made everything so unbearable that Ramazan even wanted to see Recep.

Ramazan had become accustomed to sleeping and waking next to Ali on their mattress on the floor, to lying with his nose buried in Ali's back, to breathing in the smell of forests, mountains, hillsides, rivers, soap—reminders of everything that smelled good. Ramazan's heart and soul yearned for Ali constantly. He had grown accustomed to having Ali there to make him feel clean again when he returned from work at night. This had become a need for Ramazan.

Ramazan threw himself into work. In his resentment and bitterness, he was screwing so many men that he surprised even himself that he could keep going at that rate. He saved every penny he earned: every penny.

Ramazan opened an account at a bank in Fındıkzade where he deposited cash every morning. It gave him great pleasure. He became resolute and conscientious. Ramazan hardly spent any money. He was still managing on what he had earned on Büyükada. He did not care about his appearance, had no appetite for food, and was not interested in buying material things.

Ramazan just wanted to see his bank account swell. Then, maybe, he could find a way out for them. Perhaps they could get away to another city, or even another country! The idea of starting again in another country, of starting as Ali and Ramazan all over again from zero, was so appealing that it brought tears to his eyes.

The only reason he was screwing men was to stash away money. He was creating their escape route, penny by penny, pound by pound. One day, when it was bitingly cold and Ramazan was desperate to know where Ali was and how he was managing, he bumped into Murat, a friend from the orphanage days, in Eminönü.

It turned out that Murat was living on the streets; he was a real glue head and was at rock bottom. That was what the lottery of life had dished out for him. Murat's addiction was so bad that it was impossible to tell whether his mind was in the real world or somewhere else. "Do you know where Ali is?" asked Ramazan persistently. He felt sure that Murat knew and that they inhaled together. Yes, Murat knew all right. If only he would say where Ali was. It was so cold. Where was Ali?

"Ali...? Oh, you mean Arab Ali! You should have said. Where do you stay at nights, Ramazan? You and the others? Ali? Where? Where do you sleep? Where do you go at nights?"

Eventually, after a lot of effort, Ramazan learned that Ali was sleeping in a bankomat on the main road in Çemberlitaş.

Why had not he thought of looking in the bankomats in that area? After all, they were like hotels for addicts! Ramazan could not bear to work that day. He was gripped by the idea of finding Ali and being reunited with him. His head was dizzy with excitement. Ramazan kept looking at his watch as he drank his tea. Then he went for a walk to tire himself out. He tramped along the roads from Sirkeci to Sultanahmet, up and down Çağaloğlu Slope six or seven times, and then around and around Gülhane Park. But still Ramazan could not calm his restlessness. After all these years, he still loved Ali so intensely. Was anything more important or worthwhile in life? What else did poor orphan Ramazan have in his life? As it grew dark, Ramazan went to look for the bankomat that Murat had tried so hard to describe. Ali was not there! Then, unable to stop, Ramazan went on to search all the bankomats in the area between Unkapanı and Beyazit. Ali was nowhere to be seen! He found glue heads sleeping or sitting around inhaling in a few of them, but Ali was not one of them. It was one o'clock in the morning. Ramazan's hands and feet were numb with cold, and his nose was so cold it felt as if it was about to drop off. "Just once more, Ramazan," he told himself. "Go and look in that bankomat Murat talked about one more time. If he's not there, leave it until tomorrow." Ramazan's heart was pounding as he approached the bankomat in Çemberlitaş. He had to be there! This time he was going to find Ali! He just knew Ali was there! He was certain of it.

"Ali!" Someone was lying on the floor, curled up like a fetus on top of layers of newspapers with his head between his arms and his knees drawn up to his middle. Like a baby in his mother's belly. He was bent double in an attempt to keep out the cold. Who was it? Was it Ali? Ramazan opened the door and called again, "Ali!" Ali's head moved slightly; he was so high on thinner, he could not lift it very well. But it was Ali! Yes, Ali! "Ali! My own dear Ali!" Ramazan fell to the floor and, taking Ali's head in his hands, kissed him profusely. On his eyes, his ears, his lips, and cheeks. Then he found Ali's hands, which he also covered in kisses. "Forgive me, Ali. Forgive me. Honestly, I never meant to hurt you."

"You...you must forgive me, Ramazan. I st-stabbed you. Please...forgive me. Will you? It all went wrong."

"Shush, it's not like that! Fuck you, Jungle-bear! Don't talk like that." Ramazan embraced Ali on the floor, trying to completely envelop his large body with his own. Ramazan cradled and rocked Ali as if to soothe him and send him to sleep, as if to make up for his harsh words.

"Leave me alone, Ramazan. I know it'll end badly. We're so...sooo in love. It doesn't work in this world. Doesn't wo-ork." Ali was speaking slowly and with difficulty. He still would not raise his eyes to look at Ramazan; he was afraid of giving in.

"Get up, Cave-boy! Come on, get up—we're going home. Come on! Let's go for a lovely long sleep in our bed."

"Ra-Ramazan!"

"What, Ali? Tell me. But don't say anything bad."

"Ramazan, don't forgive me."

"OK, fine. I won't forgive you, but let's go and have a good sleep. You're completely out of it. We need to get out of here. We'll escape. Everything will be all right. You'll see, Ali." Ramazan stood and pulled Ali up by his hands. Ali had difficulty remaining upright because he was so hungry, tired, and high on thinner. He was flying, but could not walk. Ramazan supported him under the arms and, very slowly, managed to get him home. Ramazan threw Ali on to the bed, took his shoes off and then his trousers. Ali's socks were stuck to his feet with blood. His feet had bled from continual walking. The blood had congealed and stuck his socks to his feet. Ramazan decided to deal with that in the morning. He threw buckets of coal into the stove. They would sleep warm that night. Ali was already asleep; he had passed out straight away. Ramazan curled up behind Ali and hugged him tightly, burying his nose in his back. Since he was a child, even on his worst days, Ali had always smelled the same. It was always a good smell to Ramazan. It was Ali. Ramazan inhaled deeply. It was lovely to be with Ali again! Like returning to paradise, or coming home. Everything felt good.

"Don't say bad things, don't even think them, Ali. We're good together, and we'll be even better. We'll go away from here, we'll escape. It won't be long now. Do you have any idea how much money I have stashed away? I haven't been idle, you know." He knew that Ali had been in a deep sleep for some time. Now he was starting to stir. It was clear that he was going through one of those bad dreams that had disturbed him since childhood. "You poor kid! And poor me! What a pair we are! Neither of us has anyone else, no one, Ali." Ramazan's eyes filled with tears; he wiped his nose with the back of his hand. Ramazan cried himself to sleep, exhausted by their situation and powerlessness, but he slept without interruption and without crows. If he did see them, he was oblivious to them. That was the best way. Is there anything better than oblivion?

DREAM 23

In his dream, Ali was in the middle of an enormous forest filled with large, majestic trees, the likes of which Ali had never seen before. Right in the middle of the forest, there was a road. It was the road that led home. Ali knew that this road would take him home, though he had no idea who the people in his dream were.

Ali's curly hair hung in ringlets down his back. "Just like when I used to take lessons from Uncle," he thought, as he awoke. "In my dream I was an innocent child, like my nine-year-old self." Uncle had taught him the Secrets. Ali was a very good student who listened and learned well, so Uncle used to give him a golden, glass-like sweet at the end of every lesson. In the middle of the sweet were bits of sesame, like magic freckles set in glass.

"We didn't have sweets like that in our village," Ali told Ramazan. "I don't know where Uncle got them from." Ali still remembered those magic sweets and those Secrets. Parts of them, not all. Sometimes he recited snatches when he was out walking.

But then things had gone wrong and his mother had become distressed. Could he have saved his mother? Was he, Ali, to blame? "The door was locked on the inside. I couldn't make her open it. And my father's relatives! I didn't think about them. I just stayed there, rooted to the spot. Oh, Mother!"

"She's in a better place, God willing," said Ramazan. Ali had never spoken of these things to him before; he tried not to remember. If he did, he did not talk about them. That morning, as he was explaining his dream, Ali started talking about his childhood. "Go on," said Ramazan, wondering what kind of dream Ali had had.

In his dream, Ali was walking alone along a lovely smooth road in the middle of the forest. It was the road home. There was still a long way to go, and it should have been impossible to see the house from where he was. But everything is different in dreams, and Ali could see the house.

An enormous Lion was standing in front of the house. A magnificent Lion with a thick, flowing mane. Lion was made of fire, and of the sun. Lion's mane shone like the sun so that it lit up the house behind. The house at the end of the road was glowing because Lion was standing in front of it. "I'm going home," Ali said in his dream. He was so happy, like a child, and even though he knew where he was going, he could not help saying, "They're waiting for me there." Lion was waiting for Ali in front of the door. Ali was unbelievably happy in his dream! Because he was going home, and because Lion was waiting for him at the door. Because the house was so beautiful, and Lion was so beautiful. "They're waiting for me," Ali said, when he told Ramazan about his dream in the morning. "I'd lost my way home, but now I've found it. My house is all lit up. Lion…" He suddenly stopped talking. Ali could not tell Ramazan about Lion. Ramazan did not know about Lion. He might say something that would make Ali feel as if he had been stabbed in the side. You could not talk about Lion to people who did not understand. Lion was a secret part of the soul. So Ali just kept saying, "I'm going home soon."

"Are you going to see your village, Ali? Are you missing it?" Ramazan no longer called Ali names like Caoutchouc, Arab-bear, Cave-boy. He knew how valuable Ali was and that he did not deserve those nicknames. Ramazan always called him Ali now, and it was clear from Ali's eyes how much he liked it. For years Ali had put up with those awful, awful nicknames. He could not help being hurt by them. Ever since the stabbing, the balance of their relationship had changed completely. Ali was now much more independent, but more introverted and withdrawn. Ali had always been withdrawn, but now there seemed to be a glaze over him, an illuminated glaze that lit up as he quietly got his life together. Ali had been calm and happy in his dreams for the last few nights. If he knew something, he was not telling Ramazan. So be it. Ramazan was the same. He did not tell Ali how much money he had saved up in the bank. It was a considerable amount of money, enough for the pair of them to get away. They could go to another country or, failing that, to another city. They could go to a warm, sunny city, for example. Ramazan was tired of damned Istanbul with its cold winters, its chilly atmosphere, and everything about it. Ramazan felt that Istanbul had fucked him up; it had fucked him up and rejected him. Now he wanted to reject Istanbul. He wanted to clear this treacherous, cruel city from his brain and his soul. "Fuck you, Istanbul!" he wanted to shout sometimes, when he was exhausted from walking through streets and parks, when he was in rooms renting himself out to men. Recently, Ramazan had started blaming Istanbul for everything bad in his life, holding it responsible for everything dirty. They would pack up and leave soon. It would not be long. In the spring, they would get the hell out of there. They would start all over again, somewhere new, completely different. "Ali and me. Me and Ali. A fresh start, with no baggage. We'll wipe the slate clean."

"I'm walking home along a road in the middle of the forest," Ali was saying. "You should see my hair, Ramazan. It was heavenly hair! So long. Our people never cut children's hair while they're having lessons with Uncle."

"What lessons?" asked Ramazan. Ali had been talking about his dream for days, a bit at a time. When Ali started explaining a bit of his dream, he would smile meaningfully. A look of such blissful happiness would cover his face that Ramazan had to let him be. Normally Ramazan would have laughed at him and tried to undermine him by saying, "What is it, you little Arab! What do you mean by all that mumbo jumbo?" But Ramazan no longer did that. He had become a different Ramazan since the stabbing. He had come to his senses. "It's better this way," thought Ramazan. "It's better if he doesn't say everything. I don't say everything either. It's better that way." Ramazan looked at Ali. Ali's eyes were the darkest eyes he had ever seen, but for days they had been illuminated as if the light of a fire were shining into them.

Or as if a fire were burning behind them. Ramazan had never seen Ali look so beautiful. Was it because he had given up thinners and all that stuff? Whatever it was, Ali was glowing and radiant. "My beautiful Ali," thought Ramazan that day as he wandered through the streets. "God loved you when he created you. He created us for each other." Ramazan was surprised to find he was missing Ali already. "We were together only an hour ago, for heaven's sake," thought Ramazan. There was something strange going on with them. What it was he did not know. If Ali knew, he was keeping quiet. "Never mind," thought Ramazan. "I've got things I'm keeping quiet about, too. So they must be good things."

COMPOSER 24

It was a crystal-clear, freezing-cold day, and the sky was a brilliant blue. The freezing cold made Ramazan's bones ache. There was no work to be had anywhere. Ramazan screwed a handsome Kurdish porter. It was hardly worth the bother, but he did it because there were no clients around.

Since Ramazan had started stashing away his money, he became nervous if he did not have four or five guys a day in order to earn reasonable money. The idea of going to the Fındıkzade branch of İş Bank the next morning with only a small amount of money to deposit was anathema to him, but even worse was the idea of having nothing at all to put in. The more Ramazan earned, the more comfortable they would be when they went away. They would have a really good start. He would make sure of that! Ramazan wandered around, in and out of beer houses. "What's going on?" he thought. "Have all the queers in bloody Istanbul dried up? Have you all had enough of getting laid? Where have you all disappeared to, you cunts?"

Ramazan downed a couple of beers, which tasted awful. He grew angry, and that famous resentment of his started to take hold. He decided to go home. Since he was already in Aksaray, it would take no time to get back to their room where he could be with Ali and they could get warm together. That idea alone was enough to cheer Ramazan up. He pulled himself together and smiled lustfully to himself.

But it was not to be! A guy suddenly appeared next to him. He was young, good-looking, well-dressed, and smelled fresh. He grinned with spotlessly clean teeth. "Hey there, rent-boy, what about it?"

Immediately Ramazan's hackles were up. If he had been a stray dog, he would have bared his molars and snarled. That sort of gay talk had always disgusted him. Right from the start, he had wanted to rid the streets of people who spoke in this way. "Are you asking how much I charge?"

"Oooh, our rent-boy is as stern as he is handsome! Let's hope he has a good ass!"

"That's enough. Piss off."

"Don't be angry, darling! I'm not your usual type, you know. I graduated from the conservatory. I'm a composer of Turkish art music." The man gave his name and started going on and on about what a great composer he was. What an important man! Ramazan was bored to death with all this talk, but he accepted the man's invitation to go and have something to eat and drink, just to get out of the cold. They walked a short distance. "Here," said the man. "Come on, let's eat and get drunk."

It was Master's wine bar! Ramazan had not set foot in the place since that last night with Master. He had always crossed the road to avoid walking past it. Yet now, here he was, walking like a lamb into that disgusting place, that terrible bar that sent him right back to the worst and most vulnerable times of his childhood. Ramazan was inside—he could not believe it. He had actually gone inside and sat down. He even started to drink.

Composer's chin never stopped wagging! He went on and on, barely stopping for breath, making Ramazan felt humiliated and crushed. Ramazan went onto autopilot. Composer droned on about what an important person he was, how strange it was that he had taken a fancy to Ramazan, and how their meeting was a stroke of luck, fate…He went on at such length that Ramazan downed four glasses of rakı in an hour, which was unheard of for him. The moment Composer saw that Ramazan was having difficulty sitting upright, he stopped his monologue and said, "Let's go back to my place to eat." Composer said that he was not feeling at all well, but that he would love Ramazan to hear some of his compositions and that he might even dedicate one of his works to him. Composer missed his child: the heartless woman with whom he had been living had taken off with his son. She had abandoned him! Composer repeated himself so often that Ramazan felt as if he were on a Ferris wheel, and the only way out was downward.

In all his years as a prostitute, Ramazan had only been in a client's house four or five times. No more than that. Ramazan found the situation extremely unpleasant and unwelcome. He was very afraid of upsetting Ali just when things were better between them, and he had no wish to hurt Ali again. But this guy was no ordinary talker. Ramazan soon found himself in a taxi heading for a residential area in Avcılar. Throughout the journey, Composer was looking into Ramazan's eyes and singing, "*Why did I love that heartless woman?*" For Ramazan, it brought back memories of his days with Master. Every so often, without interrupting the song, Composer thrust his hand out and gave Ramazan a squeeze, measuring his hardness and size. Ramazan flushed deeply at the thought that the driver might realize what was going on. He found Composer's songs and desires intolerable.

"I want the best," insisted Composer, staring at him with watery eyes. "No wham bam, thank you ma'am, my dear Ramo. We'll be together until morning. I'm a man of love, a man of music. I'm not your ordinary queen type. No, I'm not like them, I'm a man." Ramazan felt uncomfortable and embarrassed, and he began to sweat profusely. Every so often, he caught the driver eyeing them through the rearview mirror with a dirty grin. He was obviously going to enjoy a good hand job after dropping them off. Ramazan decided to stay in the taxi with the driver, whatever the cost. If necessary he would draw his knife and stick it in Composer. Ramazan had absolutely no intention of entering Composer's domain, putting up with any more of his bragging or being further humiliated. He would not be made a monkey of in a stranger's home. Everything about Composer, his watery fish-like eyes and his hands, reminded him of Master. Taking him to Master's wine bar, singing songs to him, and making advances to him like that was more than Ramazan could bear. Much more.

"We're here! This is my little hovel. Turn right and stop in front of the first apartment block please, driver."

The driver turned right round to face them. "Of course, sir. As you say," he said. "Thank you for all the music. I'm sure there's a lot more where that came from!"

Ramazan could contain himself no longer. "Just get out," he yelled at Composer. Ramazan realized that his rage had reached the point of no return, and he was on the verge of killing the guy.

"But Ramo…" said Composer, trying to calm Ramazan as he sent the driver away. Then his manner changed, and he adopted a more persuasive and effective tone. "I'm a man," he said to Ramazan, looking at him with his watery fish eyes. "Two days ago, I sold my brand-new Renault, so I swear on my mother's life that I have stacks of money. Come upstairs and soothe this crazy heart of mine. I'll give you more money than you make in a month. And you'll also have the time of your life." He winked, put out his tongue, and licked his lips.

Ramazan was stranded there in the middle of the night at the entrance to an apartment building. How could he walk all the way back in that cold? He had been freezing to death for hours as it was, and there would be no buses or anything running at that hour of night. And what had old moneybags said? The sort of money he had mentioned was more than Ramazan could make in two or three months, especially if the winter continued like this. "What have I got to lose?" said Ramazan. "I'll go up to his apartment, screw this bastard all night, then in the morning, I'll pocket a wad of notes and go home. Maybe, I won't have to work again, and Ali and I might even get away before spring. I've had enough of all this."

"Are you muttering prayers, my little homo? Ooh, you're like a tasty little child, you're so cute! Come and screw me to make me feel better. Wipe away my tears. Then do it again and again." Composer started to laugh. "But I mean it. Are you afraid I'm not up to it? My equipment's in very good order. Just come up and see." Composer laughed manically, interspersing his laughter with crazy-sounding words.

A window opened on the third floor, and a middle-aged woman looked out at them before quickly shutting the window. She looked frightened, as if she understood instantly what was going to happen. Ramazan felt deeply ashamed again. "Oh, whatever," he said to himself. "Go inside, do what you have to do. This will be the last time. Never again." That is exactly what he said to himself. "This'll be the last," thought Ramazan. The chain of prostitution that had started with Master would end with Composer, who reminded Ramazan so much of Master. This would be his means of escape. It was with these thoughts that he entered the apartment. Composer was already unzipping his fly while they were in the elevator. Ramazan remained silent. "He's had it, I've got his number," thought Ramazan. "This is the last time, the very last time." Ramazan was instantly as hard as a rod. He had never once dropped his professional standards. Ramazan immediately felt good. He entered the fellow's mouth to stop him talking. He felt even better.

Now Ramazan was in control. That was just fine. Everything was as it should be.

NIGHT 25

There was vodka, beer, and banana liqueur in the apartment. They drank everything. They drank and they screwed. Composer could not get enough. "Let's do it over there. Let's do it this way. Come on, my homo, my lovely boy!"

Ramazan could not remember ever working so hard in one night, inside and out. In between screwing sessions, they kept on drinking and the man kept on talking. Composer cried over his son and railed against the child's mother. He slated her continually, without ever mentioning her name, not even once. Ramazan remembered Doormat—what she had suffered and what they had inflicted on her. Every so often, Composer went to his electric keyboard and sang one of his songs in a high-pitched whining voice that reminded Ramazan of Master. He sang "My Only Love" at least half a dozen times. Composer kept looking into Ramazan's eyes as if he were dying of love and had written that song especially for him. To shut the fellow up, to stop his talking and crying, to stop him going to the keyboard and playing his song all over again, Ramazan even took him in his own mouth.

That was something he had never before done with clients, only with Ali. Only with Ali—when he thought of his Ali, Ramazan could take no more. He pulled himself away and spat.

The man still kept talking in a voice that seemed to penetrate right through Ramazan. Composer entered Ramazan's mouth again and made him keep sucking to the end, while Composer shouted and writhed about. Ramazan finally managed to extricate himself and made a dash for the toilet. He was smoldering with resentment, and his rage had reached boiling point, but he was confused and unable to think clearly.

Ramazan could not pull himself together, either physically or mentally. He had drunk too much and spent too long screwing and listening to drivel. He had become too cold and tired, and the final straw was that he been reminded of the past. Finally, Composer led Ramazan by the hand into the bedroom. Ramazan did not have the strength to protest or pull his hand away.

Composer threw Ramazan on to the bed, leapt on top of him, and began screwing him. "This can't be real," thought Ramazan. "It's just a bad dream. A dirty dream. It's not real. It can't be happening."

Ramazan was not sure exactly how much time passed, but it must have been several hours. He woke up to wings flapping in his face. A flock of crows was flying around his head, flapping their wings. They were very, very close. It was the weight of those wings that woke Ramazan. The wings were beating so close to his nose and mouth that he could not breathe. Ramazan was suffocating as the crows flapped their wings.

Ramazan opened his eyes and saw Composer lying in a comatose state with his head on Ramazan's arm. He looked down at the fellow's lower body, then at his own. Ramazan was filled with self-loathing. He felt such disgust with himself, at what they had done and at the creature lying next to him that he felt like cutting off his own penis.

Quietly and carefully, Ramazan got out of the bed, his heart pounding with fear that the fellow might wake up. Never before had Ramazan encountered anyone with such hunger, greed, and lust. "He promised to pay so much," thought Ramazan. "But I bet he pays shit money! There's no way this bastard will pay what he promised. He'll just start whining and singing again." Ramazan looked fearfully at Composer, who was still in a deep sleep.

Ramazan had never felt captive like this before, except for when he was with Master. And then he had been a mere child, a slip of a boy, a poor orphan of unknown origin. Ramazan's eyes welled up when he thought of his childhood. He just wanted to sit there and cry for his lost childhood, his fucked-up childhood, and to throttle Master with his hands, squeeze his throat tight.

Picking his pants up from the floor, Ramazan looked over at the fellow. Why did he remind him so much of Master? Composer was a handsome young man, but seeing him lying unconscious there made Ramazan's stomach heave. Ramazan put on his underpants and realized the back of them was sticky. The bastard had actually screwed him. It was not a just nightmare. He had fucked the hell out of Ramazan! Composer's pants were lying on the floor. Ramazan put them on over his own pants. He went to empty the pockets, which he knew would be full of cash.

But they were not. The fellow had promised more than that. There had to be more; otherwise Ramazan would never forgive himself. After all, he had come here to make money. The cunt had been having Ramazan on! Ramazan went into the living room to look for Composer's jacket. He pulled it out from under one of the cushions and put it on over his own jacket.

The pockets were full of cash, just as Ramazan had expected. He looked around the room for a couple of things he could take to sell so that he would at least feel he had gotten what he deserved—although actually, nothing could repay him for that night. The fellow had fucked him! It should not have happened. And he had made Ramazan take him in his mouth—made him do everything. Ramazan had never ever been in a situation like that before.

There was a good collection of videos, which Ramazan stuffed under his arm. That was enough—he was already weighted down with the two pairs of pants and two jackets he was wearing. "Goddamn him," Ramazan said to himself. "Son of a bitch!" He had a splitting headache and felt very sick. As soon as he got out of this apartment, he would have a good vomit. Whatever was inside him, he would throw up, and how! Ramazan went over to the front door and turned the doorknob. Shit! The apartment door would not open. He tried it a few more times. The fellow had locked the door—so what now? "Hell!" said Ramazan. "Is there no getting away from you? Are you a pimp, or what?" He gave the door a good shake. But there was no point!

"What's going on, my little ram?" Composer had woken up, and he was calling from the bedroom. But his voice was different. It was a stern, masculine voice that was both questioning and threatening.

Ramazan immediately thrust his hand into his pocket. The switchblade was not there! Perhaps he could not find it because he was wearing two jackets. But no, the switchblade was not there! The fellow must have locked the door, hidden the key, and taken the switchblade after Ramazan had passed out. He had taken care of everything! "What a bastard!" said Ramazan, aloud this time.

Like a cat, he leapt into the kitchen and grabbed a large knife that was lying on the worktop. Ramazan came out of the kitchen and immediately came face to face with Composer.

"What do you think you're doing, you little tart?"

"You're the tart. I hope you die in hell," said Ramazan, or he thought he did. His eyes went black with anger. But now, Ramazan found himself looking in disbelief at Composer, who had fallen in front of the keyboard and was convulsing like a dying earthworm on the floor. Ramazan could not believe he had cut him open like that! The enormous knife had entered just below the chest and gone down through the stomach and out the other side. Composer was lanced open, his belly slit in half! His intestines had spilled out and were heaped on the floor next to him. Had Ramazan done this? Was it so easy? Had he actually done this, too? Ramazan rushed out onto the balcony, thinking his only option was to climb down from there and get away. There was no other option—but how would he do it? "How are you going to get out of this, Ramazan? Shit, you've really done it this time!" He was scared of going back into the living room and seeing Composer lying there with his guts all over the floor. Ramazan was shitting himself with fear and dread when he suddenly noticed a cable on the balcony. It was an antenna cable. Great! He pulled the cable out of the antenna and fastened it tightly to the balcony railing. Once, then twice, three, four more times, he tied it with trembling hands. Thank God, the cable was really long! The apartment was on the sixth floor, and the cable reached right down to the ground. "Sixth floor, for fuck's sake! But there's no other way, Ramazan!" Ramazan climbed over the railings so that he was now outside the balcony. He grabbed the cable and slid downward like a monkey. Ramazan remembered the tree in the courtyard and how Ali used to climb up it like a cat and sit there in a sort of trance. "Oh, Ali." Daylight was breaking. "That's good," thought Ramazan. "Ali! My Ali, could you sleep without me?" Ramazan's last thought was of Ali. The cable snapped, fifteen centimeters below all those knots. The cable snapped, and Ramazan crashed from the sixth floor onto the concrete below.

He died instantly.

MORNING 26

A sixty-five-year-old eyewitness, who took a daily early morning walk around the apartment block, stated:

As I was walking round the block that morning, I heard a big commotion. Then the police arrived. The police would not allow anyone near the area where the body was found beneath the balcony, but I was very close. A few uniformed police searched the man's clothes. He was wearing two pairs of trousers and two jackets. A policeman took a handful of marks from the trouser pockets and put them into his own pocket.

December 1992—Hürriyet

Ramazan had not come home that night. And Ramazan did not come home the next morning. Ramazan should have returned because he always came home. He would be back any minute. He must be on his way back to their room, Ali and Ramazan's room.

It was Monday, the seventh of December, and Ali felt immobilized by an arrow pressing against his side. It was an enormously long arrow. Whichever way he turned, he came up against it. Whatever he did, even when lying down, the pain would not go away. If Ali pulled the arrow out, it would disappear, leaving no trace of blood; but that huge arrow in his side did not allow him to so much as stir.

Ali spent the day of Monday, the seventh of December, hardly able to breathe with worry and angst. He was pierced to the core by the arrow.

On Tuesday, the eighth of December, they brought the newspapers to Ali. His glue head friends brought them to him at about noon. The papers were full of pictures of Ramazan. Certain pages were covered with pictures of Ramazan—Ali's Ramazan. There was one really large picture showing Ramazan lying on the concrete, in the patterned sweater he had been wearing when he left home. Ali stared long and hard at that sweater. As if, provided he kept staring at the sweater, he would not see Ramazan's face covered in blood. Ramazan's beautiful face covered in blood. They had covered his face and lower half with newspapers. But later, somebody had pulled the newspapers up over his forehead to reveal his face.

Thus, one hundred thousand people, including Ali, especially Ali, saw Ramazan's face covered in blood. But Ali did not see. Right next to Ramazan lay five meters of antenna cable, coiled up like a snake. The fifteen centimeters of antenna cable that had been found tied to the balcony railing matched the five meters of cable on the ground. The papers recounted all this in great detail. The papers had also taken a picture of the bloodied face from above.

Ali was not spared any of the details. Ali read without reading. He saw without seeing. His mind could not take it all in. Everything was a blur and he understood nothing. But Ramazan had died. That had been the arrow in Ali's side; that much he knew. If Ramazan was not there, then that was it. One of the papers wrote:

Since no one has come forward to claim the corpse,
it is being held at Adli Tıp Morgue.

Ramazan had become a corpse. Nobody wanted Ramazan's corpse. The corpse was at the morgue. But Ali wanted Ramazan's corpse, every bit of it. Ali wanted to go and kiss every part of Ramazan's beautiful bloodstained head. He accepted Ramazan in any state, always had. But Ali knew he could not be reunited with Ramazan in that way. Even if he went along and kissed Ramazan's corpse, Ali would still be alive. Ali would be here, and Ramazan would be there. Ali knew that the arrow that had pierced him, whether it was three, five, or fifteen meters long, would be with him always. That arrow had come between them. Ramazan was now there, and Ali was here.

Ali sat motionlessly in their room all that day and the following night. His glue head friends resorted to solvents to avoid feeling pain. To pills and drink. Ali had already come to terms with the situation. Ramazan had gone. Gone. Gone. The Ramazan of Ali and Ramazan had gone. He had fallen from a balcony. The cable had snapped. Ramazan had crashed to the ground. First he was on the ground, now he was in the morgue. He was waiting for Ali. Ali kept saying, "Ramazan is waiting for me. Ramazan's waiting." The glue heads continued inhaling thinners. Finally, it occurred to one of them to burn the newspapers in the stove. Ali cried out as the newspapers burned. "Ramazan! Ramazaaaaaan!" Ali started to weep as the papers burned in the stove. He wept until morning. He wept and kept repeating, "Ramazan's waiting for me." The boys would not leave Ali on his own. Ali was in a dangerous state and was very likely to do something to himself.

Ali said nothing to them. But he still had one more thing of beauty in his life. Lion was waiting for him. His fiery mane was visible in front of the house at the end of the road. Lion was waiting for him. In front of his house.

Lion was allowing him to return home. His home had forgiven Ali. His mother was at home, and Ramazan was there. Anyone Ali had loved was there. And whom had Ali loved? His dear mother. His Ramazan. "*Yemoooo! Yemoooo!*" howled Ali, yearning for his mother. Ali had never stopped missing his mother for a single moment of a single day.

The next morning, Ali seemed his normal self again. "Let's go to the hostel together," he begged the boys. They had been in the habit of visiting the building site in Bakırköy, where a new orphanage was being constructed. They used to wander around there looking at the building work.

The building work was progressing month by month, year by year. The very State that had put them out in the street was now building a brand-new orphanage for new children. "Hey, this is luxury! Remember our old school building?" they said. For months, they had frequented the new building as if, when finished, this State-owned hostel would take them in again, as if there were a place for them. They were obsessed by the new hostel and had to keep going back for yet another look. Ali pleaded and begged until, finally, the boys gave in, and they set off for the building site. This time, Ali said, "Let's break a window and go inside. We can sleep here." The boys agreed, thinking Ali did not know what he was saying or doing. But some watchmen spotted the three of them and called the police.

Ali spent the night of December 9 in a police station making a statement that he had tried to break into the Şeyh Sait Children's Nursery, which was under construction in the garden of the Bakırköy Orphanage Hostel. That is how Ali spent that night.

Ramazan was waiting for him, and Ali was late. Lion, with his fiery mane, was waiting for Ali in front of his house.

THE HOSTEL 27

On December 10, 1992, Ali went alone to the building site at Bakırköy Children's Home. Very quietly and carefully. He knew exactly where he wanted to go. He walked to where the children's nursery was being built and waited until it grew dark. He was totally alone. In his pocket, he had some rope that he had bought from a hardware store. He selected a window. Rolling his jacket into a ball, he leaned against the window. He put his fist through and shattered the glass. Ali was still powerfully strong. He broke the adjacent window, too, and pushed it in. He climbed inside. New orphans would be cared for here. Outside was written: *Şeyh Sait Children's Nursery*. Lots of children would live at the nursery. Lots of children would live in this beautiful hostel when the building was finished. Ali had been watching its construction for months. He would have liked to see it finished. "It wasn't to be," he said to himself.

Tying the rope carefully, he placed it deliberately round his neck. He did everything very slowly and carefully. He had not inhaled any thinner that day. His head was absolutely clear.

Crystal clear. "Ramazan!" he said, as if Ramazan could hear him. But Ali knew he would hear. "You remember how I always used to cry for my mother every night. I wouldn't have survived without you, Ramazan. I couldn't have survived. You saved me. With you…" He fell silent, choking with sorrow. Ramazan must not wait for him any longer. It was always Ali who waited for Ramazan. Ramazan was not used to waiting. He did not know how to wait for anyone. It was something he had never learned. Ali laughed. He was laughing at Ramazan's impatience, his vitality, everything about him. "You were the only person to make me happy. You made me into Ali: the Ali of Ali and Ramazan."

Ali put the noose round his neck and hanged himself on the nursery building site at about eight o'clock in the evening. As his body slackened, a marble fell from his hand and rolled along the ground. "The marble's yours. You're my type, Ali." These were the last words that passed through Ali's mind as he clutched the marble he had taken from his pocket. But he remembered Ramazan's words as, "You're with me, Ali. Take it, it's yours."

"I'll always be with you," Ali said. "I'll be with you forever, Ramazan." These were the words Ali said before he died. Aliiiiiiiiiii! Aliiiiiiiiiii!

END